# Bad Chemistry

What do you do when your new chemistry teacher is arrested on a charge of murder? If you're Frank and Joe Hardy you set to work straight away to get her off the hook. Yvonne Ziebarth has left her research job at a university and taken up teaching. The trouble is the job isn't the only thing she left behind – she left a dead boss too! But it seems to Frank and Joe this case has all the elements of a frame-up. It's time to do some research of their own and their findings . . . could be fatal!

# HARDY BOYS™

# Bad Chemistry

POCKET
BOOKS

POCKET
B O O K S

An imprint of Simon & Schuster UK Ltd
Africa House, 64-78 Kingsway
London WC2B 6AH

ISBN 0 671 77348 8

1 3 5 7 9 10 8 6 4 2

Printed by Caledonian International Book Manufacturing, Glasgow

This book was originally published in Great Britain
as an ARCHWAY PAPERBACK number 110

All Pocket Books are available by post from:
**Simon & Schuster Cash Sales**.
PO Box 29, Douglas, Isle of Man IM99 1BQ
Credit cards accepted.
Please telephone 01624 836000
fax 01624 670923, Internet
http://www.bookpost.co.uk or email:
bookshop@enterprise.net for details

# Chapter

## 1

FENTON HARDY WAS knotting his tie as he strode into the kitchen. The former New York City police officer, now a private detective, was in a hurry to meet a client, but the scene at the breakfast table stopped him in his tracks. His younger son, Joe, was hunched over what appeared to be a chemistry textbook next to a plate of eggs.

"Joe, are you okay?" Fenton asked, with a wink at his wife, Laura, who was pouring fresh orange juice into four tall glasses.

"Oh—morning, Dad," Joe said, looking up. A junior in high school, Joe was six feet tall with an athletic build. He had blond hair and blue eyes. This morning he looked particularly sharp in a short-sleeved shirt, a neat pair of jeans, and new sneakers.

"Now, Fenton," Laura said, pretending to scold her husband, "we don't want to discourage the boy from doing his schoolwork, do we?"

"Of course not," Fenton said, "but it is a bit of a shock to see him working on chemistry equations first thing in the morning."

"They're not equations, Dad," Joe said. "These are application forms. I'm checking into summer school programs. Bayport U. has a chemistry course that takes only six weeks, but I'd get a full term of high school credit. Or I might try for a summer internship at a drug company."

Fenton Hardy turned to his wife. "Honey, did you hear that? Joe Hardy's going to spend his summer in a chemistry lab. What I'm concerned about is what it's going to do to his plans for a professional baseball career."

"Easy, Fenton," said Laura Hardy as she sprinkled shredded cheese over a second batch of eggs she was scrambling in a skillet. Together with the onions already sizzling, they filled the room with delicious smells. "We aren't supposed to be making fun of him. We're supposed to be encouraging him."

"You're right as usual," Fenton said, turning to his son. "So, Joe, why the sudden interest in chemistry?"

"That's easy," Frank Hardy said as he walked in. Frank was a year older than his

2

brother and a senior at Bayport High. Standing six-foot-one, with brown hair and brown eyes, he was built like a wide receiver. "It isn't the chemistry," Frank said. "It's the new chemistry *teacher.*"

"Frank!" Joe said. "Do you mind?"

"*Yvonne* Ziebarth," Frank said, raising his eyebrows.

"Frank, grow up," Joe said.

"Other than her name," Fenton Hardy said, "is there any reason your new teacher is so interesting?"

"Dad," Frank answered for Joe, "if you saw her you'd understand. Yvonne Ziebarth doesn't look like your average chemistry teacher—that is, unless your average chemistry teacher is a tall, slim, beautiful twenty-five-year-old with long red hair and green eyes. Have I forgotten anything, Joe?"

Joe glared at his brother. "You forgot to mind your own business."

"Why do you have a new teacher so late in the term?" Fenton asked.

"Mrs. Crosby left on maternity leave," Joe explained. "Ms. Ziebarth's filling in."

"She was available in the middle of the term?" their father asked, sipping his coffee. "What was she doing before?"

Frank turned toward his brother. "Yeah, what's the story, Joe? You must know all the details."

3

"Ms. Ziebarth was a grad student at Bayport University," Joe said. "For some reason she quit. She started to tell us one day, but the bell rang and she never got to it."

"And what does Vanessa think of all this?" Laura Hardy asked.

Vanessa Bender was a new girl in town when Joe met her. From the start he liked her looks, intelligence, wit, and independent ways. They had been dating ever since.

"Oh, I think Vanessa understands," answered Frank, helping himself to the eggs. "She realizes this is just a one-sided infatuation—like a little kid with a crush."

Joe suddenly stood and whisked his dishes off the table and to the sink. "I'm out of here," he said.

Frank grinned as he buttered a piece of toast. "Mom? Dad? Do you want to take a wild guess what Joe's first class is?"

Joe scooped up his application forms, shoved them into his book bag, and walked out the door. "Frank, I've got the keys," he called over his shoulder. "In exactly two minutes I'm going to be backing down the driveway. So unless you want to walk to school, you'd better stick that toast in your pocket and get out to the van."

Joe pulled their black van into the Bayport High School parking lot and found a space near the side entrance. "Man, wouldn't you know we'd get caught in traffic," Joe said as he yanked on the hand brake. Then he punched his seat belt release, grabbed his books, and snatched at the door handle.

"Traffic?" Frank said, climbing out. "We waited thirty seconds for a cop to wave us around a stalled car."

The sky was clear and bright, promising a warm day. Summer was just around the corner.

"I just don't want to be late, that's all."

"Joe, we're twenty minutes early. The place is deserted. We just got the best parking space in the entire lot." Joe was marching double time toward the door, and even Frank was having a hard time keeping up.

"Well, if I hadn't had to wait while you blabbered instead of eating your breakfast—"

Frank stopped to pluck at the front of his T-shirt. "Hey, I've got crumbs all down my shirt from chewing cold toast in the van, you maniac."

"Listen," Joe called back over his shoulder, "if you're going to hang around out here, I'll meet you later, okay?"

"Have a good time in class," Frank called as Joe pulled on the big green door and went inside. "Try looking at the blackboard once in a while, too."

Joe trotted up the hallway, his sneakers squeaking on the tile floor. Frank was wrong.

The place wasn't totally deserted—other students were already there. Joe poked his head inside the door of the chemistry classroom and saw two figures slumped forward on their desks with heads down on their forearms, catching a few extra winks. There was no teacher yet though. He turned and hurried down the hall to the door marked Boys.

After noisily dropping his books onto a sink counter, Joe whipped out a comb from his back pocket and ran it across his head. Satisfied, he dug a silver cylinder the size of a roll of dimes out of his pocket, peeled off a breath mint, and popped it into his mouth. He hesitated, popped two more mints in his mouth, then rushed out.

At the classroom door he took a deep, pepperminty breath and walked in.

Yvonne Ziebarth stood at the front of the room, her attendance book clutched in one hand, a pen in the other. She had begun calling roll and was down to the *H*'s when Joe walked in. She looked up and smiled. Her green eyes were sparkling as she said, "Joe Hardy, right on time."

Joe was starting to blurt out "Present!" but he choked on his breath mints, and the only sound that came out of his mouth was a loud cough. Ziebarth and the other students stared, but Joe waved them all off, smiling while he tried to stifle a gag. Instead, he swallowed a throatful of peppermint and let out a barrage of coughs and gags. So much for smooth entrances, he thought.

"Joe, the essay questions on your exam were really fine," Ms. Ziebarth said.

Joe and his favorite teacher were walking down the hall at the end of the day. It was almost five o'clock, but Joe had stayed late to talk about chemistry with Ms. Ziebarth after she finished grading papers. Joe proudly clutched the exam, which he had aced. As far as he was concerned, his embarrassing entrance that morning was ancient history.

"In fact," Ziebarth continued, "I photocopied the exam to show my other class." She showed him the copy, which was clipped to the cover of her attendance book.

"I did study a lot," Joe admitted. "Actually, I'm thinking about a summer chemistry course or maybe an internship."

"Why don't you walk me out to my car?" she said. "I got a flyer about an internship in the mail yesterday. I think I filed it in the backseat of my car."

Joe was wrapped up in the conversation, but still he noticed the two men in dark suits and ties standing outside Ms. Ziebarth's office down the hall. He began to say something about them when she turned and ducked out the door to the parking lot. Joe followed but not before taking in the expressions of surprise on the men's faces.

As they stepped outside and walked up to Ms. Ziebarth's car, Joe heard a police siren in the background. "By the way," he started to say, "outside your office door—"

"How about this weather?" she cut in, drawing in a deep breath of fresh air. "I can't wait for summer."

"Me neither," Joe said. The police siren was getting louder.

"Here we are," Ms. Ziebarth said, her keys in her hand as she approached a small white sedan in the teachers' parking area.

As Ms. Ziebarth leaned over the front seat to check for the flyer in the back, Joe saw two patrol cars racing up the street toward them.

"I wonder what that's all about," Ms. Ziebarth said as she straightened up. "Looks like they're turning in here."

The patrol cars split up and sped down different aisles, red lights flashing and sirens shrieking. A touch football game on the front lawn stopped in midplay, and everyone turned to watch. Cars on the street slowed down to catch a glimpse of what sort of trouble might be brewing at the high school. The driver of one patrol car sped past them, then hit the brakes, tires squealing, and backed up fast.

"They're backing right up to us," Ziebarth

said, checking to see if anyone else was nearby. "What is this?"

Joe heard a school door bang open and then clang shut. He turned to see the two men in suits—one big and burly, the other small and wiry—come charging out.

Meanwhile, the patrol car rocked to a hard stop behind Ziebarth's white car, blocking any escape.

"Freeze!" the bigger man shouted as he jogged up to them. "Police."

A revolver gleamed in his fist, and his other hand brushed back his jacket to reveal a gold detective's shield attached to his belt. His partner, close behind, stopped and assumed the classic two-handed firing stance.

"Don't move a muscle," the first man said. "Yvonne Ziebarth, you are under arrest."

# Chapter

## 2

NEITHER JOE NOR HIS TEACHER moved. Joe had a hard time believing what was happening. He wanted to protest, but he knew it was best to keep quiet and not move.

"Thought you'd make a run for it, did you?" the bigger of the two detectives said.

"What am I under arrest for?" Ziebarth said. "This must be some kind of mistake."

"No mistake if you're Yvonne Ziebarth," the big man said. "I'm Detective Broussard, Bayport Police, and I've got a warrant for your arrest." He pulled a pair of handcuffs out from his jacket.

"You don't really have to put those on her, do you?" Joe asked.

The detective spun toward Joe. "All right, fella, who are you?"

"Joe Hardy. I'm a student here."

"Hardy. Any relation to Fenton Hardy the detective?"

"He's my father," Joe said.

"Well, don't think that gives you the right to interfere. We're conducting police business here that doesn't concern you. So move along."

"But, Detective Broussard—" Joe said.

"Move along, son," Broussard said. "You heard what I said."

In a few short moments a small crowd had gathered around them. The two detectives were obviously concerned with one thing and one thing only: bringing their captive in without causing any more commotion.

"I'm sorry, ma'am, but you'll have to come with us," Broussard said. He and his partner each grabbed Ziebarth by an elbow and led her to their unmarked car.

As she was led away, Joe caught a glimpse of the expression on Ms. Ziebarth's face. It was equal parts confusion and fear. He could hear Broussard start to recite her her rights. "You have the right to remain silent, you have the right . . ." Then he heard a familiar voice from the back of the crowd.

"Joe—hey, Joe! What's going on?" Frank asked. He had stayed late, too, to catch up on some work in the library.

"You won't believe it," Joe said. "Two detectives just arrested Ms Ziebarth."

"Fill me in on the way home," Frank said, turning to walk toward their van. "Mom's roasting a turkey, and I don't want to be late for dinner." As they were climbing into their van, the detectives locked Ms. Ziebarth in the backseat of the unmarked car, got in, and took off.

As Frank drove, Joe raised his voice over the warm air rushing through the van's open windows. He barely noticed the scenery skimming past as he described the afternoon's events.

"A teacher arrested right on school property," Frank said, shaking his head in amazement. "Bayport High'll remember that scene for a long time to come. What exactly was it all about?"

"I wish I knew. I mean, they sort of edged me out. But it was definitely something major—"

"Something major involving a chemistry teacher? I don't think so, Joe. Maybe a parking ticket or jaywalking."

"Frank," Joe said, "they were going to slap cuffs on her."

"They were?" Frank glanced sideways at his brother. "I guess it could be pretty serious."

"And before they hustled her off in the d-car"—Frank noted Joe's use of the police term for a detective's car—"they read her her rights."

"Then what?" Frank asked.

"That's it. Let's give Con Riley a call after dinner." Officer Riley was the Hardys' best contact in the Bayport Police Department. Although department regulations wouldn't allow Con to cooperate with the boys officially, he always tried to help. Often he had valuable information to offer them.

By the time they got home, dinner was almost ready. They had just enough time to stow their gear and wash up.

Joe helped by carrying the hot stuffed turkey into the dining room. Frank followed with a casserole of string beans and potatoes. Fenton and Laura Hardy settled in quickly at the table. The boys' aunt Gertrude was away for a couple of days.

"Mom, Dad, do you remember my chemistry teacher?" Joe said as he sat down. "The one we were talking about this morning? Well, after school today—"

*Brr-r-r-ring!*

"Right on cue," Laura said, getting up to answer the hall telephone, which always seemed to ring the minute they sat down for dinner. "I wonder what it would be like for this family to have a hot meal for once."

"Sorry, Laura," Fenton said. "If it's for me, I'll call back later—"

The next moment they heard her voice in the hallway. "Hardy residence . . . Yes, that's right. . . ."

"Dad," Joe began again. "What I was trying to say was that after school I was leaving the building with Ms. Ziebarth—"

"Fenton?" Laura called.

"Yes, dear?"

Laura Hardy came into the room, obviously concerned. "It's"—she glanced at Joe—"Yvonne Ziebarth. She says it's important. She apologized for calling at dinnertime, but she can't choose when to call. She's at the police station."

"What?" asked Fenton Hardy.

"She got arrested, Dad. That's what I was trying to tell you," Joe said.

Fenton Hardy laid his napkin on the table and stood up. "Well, let's see what this is all about." He went out to the hallway and picked up the receiver.

"Hello, Ms. Ziebarth," he said. "Yes . . . yes, I know somebody who could help you out. She's one of the best criminal lawyers in Bayport. Let me get her number for you. Hold on a second, it's in my office." Fenton put the receiver down and said, "Joe, do you want to talk to her while I go look up a number for her?"

"Thanks, Dad." Joe came out and got on the phone. "Ms. Ziebarth?"

"Joe. Oh, it's good to hear a familiar voice."

"What's happening?"

There was a long pause on the line. Then Yvonne Ziebarth let out a quiet whistle and said, "Joe, I'm not sure. All I know is I'm under arrest for murder."

"Murder?" Joe echoed.

"It's a nightmare. My ex-boss at Bayport University was killed in a lab accident. You may have read about it in the paper the other day."

"Professor Thomas Klingner, sure," Joe said. "You worked for him?"

Ziebarth hesitated. "Actually, I'm not sure I should be telling you all this."

"Ms. Ziebarth, I don't know if you know this, but my brother and I do detective work. We may be able to help you out."

Joe's teacher hesitated again. "Well, this'll probably all be in the papers tomorrow anyway. Joe, they're blaming me. They're saying I murdered Dr. Klingner."

"That's crazy."

"Anyway, they told me I could call a lawyer, but I don't know any. My family's back in Wisconsin. An officer here—his name's Con Riley—said he's a friend of you and your brother's."

"Con's a good guy," Joe said. "You can trust him."

"Well, he noticed your name on that copy of the exam clipped to my attendance book, so he suggested I call your father. He said he'd know a good lawyer."

"But if Klingner's death was an accident . . .?"

"No, the police think it was murder. He died of phosgene poisoning."

"Phosgene?" Joe said.

"Poisonous gas. Very dangerous stuff. There was an open canister of it clutched in Klingner's hand when they found him.'"

"So why do they think it was murder? Couldn't it have been an accident?"

"The canister had a phony label saying it was oxygen," Ziebarth said.

"And why do they think you did it?"

"Because the label was printed on my old computer," Ziebarth said, "in my old office, next door to the lab."

"Seems like pretty flimsy evidence," Joe said as Fenton came in from the other room holding a slip of paper. "Ms. Ziebarth, I'm sure things will work out. Here's my dad again."

"Thanks, Joe. I may call on you and your brother."

When Fenton sat back down to the lukewarm plate of food, he said, "There's not much else we can do for her tonight. Let's finish dinner and see how things shape up tomorrow."

The next day when the Bayport High lunch bell rang, Joe made a beeline from his classroom to the school library.

Because of his newfound interest in chemistry, Joe was familiar with the science section. It didn't take him long to find several chemistry texts that included sections on phosgene.

He spent the next twenty minutes reading about the gas, a mixture of chlorine and carbon monoxide that had first been used as a weapon during World War I. Released over the trenches, it killed soldiers quickly by turning to hydrofluoric acid in their lungs. Phosgene's distinctive smell of fresh-mown grass was the last thing its victims ever sensed.

Joe stopped to wonder if there were any survivors of a phosgene attack. Closing the book, Joe turned his thoughts to Ms. Ziebarth. He refused to believe she was a murderer. If Dr. Thomas Klingner *had* died of foul play, someone else must have been responsible—and Joe vowed that he would help find out who it was.

"Frank. Hey, Frank!" Joe yelled.

Amid the crowd of students swarming from school after last period, Frank spotted his brother waving. He made his way over to Joe and said, "You going to baseball practice?"

Joe drew up beside his brother. "Actually, I'm going to cut. I had something else in mind. What do you say we head down to the police station to see what we can find out to help Ms. Ziebarth?"

"I don't know, Joe."

"I just know she wouldn't do something like this. She's innocent and somebody is trying to get away with murder. Come on, what do you say? I'll owe you one."

Frank frowned. "All right, I guess baseball can wait."

At Bayport Police Headquarters the Hardys made their way inside hoping to see Officer Con Riley. Approaching the desk sergeant seated high above them, Frank craned his neck to look up and said, "Excuse me, sir. Is Officer Riley in yet?" The brothers had phoned ahead that morning and learned Riley was on the night shift, which ran from four to midnight. Most officers arrived a half hour or so before their shift. They changed in the locker room, checked their equipment, and chatted with friends finishing up the day shift.

"Riley?" the large, bald-headed desk sergeant repeated. "Let me check." He ran a thick finger along a row of names and sign-in times in his notebook. "Yeah, he just got in. Your names?"

"Frank and Joe Hardy," said Frank.

The sergeant picked up a telephone and called Riley. After he hung up and said, "He'll be right out," it was no more than a minute before Con Riley appeared. In freshly pressed "blues" and shined shoes, he was ready for work. "Hi, fellas. What can I do for you?"

"We're here about the Klingner case, Con,"

said Joe. "Yvonne Ziebarth called us last night after she was arrested."

"Sure, I suggested she call you," Riley said. "What a surprise. We don't get a lot of high school teachers arrested for murder. You're in one of her classes, right, Joe?"

"Yep, she just started," Joe said. "Can you tell us anything about the case?"

"Now, just a minute," Riley said. "You can't expect any help from me—you know the official policy. You have to talk to the detectives assigned to this case. Henry Broussard's one."

"Is he here?"

"I'm afraid not," Riley said. "I saw him go out a few minutes ago."

"Con, I know the official policy," Frank said, "but could you just tell us about the evidence against Ms. Ziebarth? That can't be too secret."

"There's not much," Con said, checking to see if anyone was listening in. "Most of it you'll probably read in the papers tomorrow. Looks like somebody switched the label on a canister filled with the gas that killed him. We know Ziebarth was Klingner's assistant while she was working for her doctorate degree. We also know they had a big falling-out. That's when she left the university and started teaching at the high school."

"A big falling-out?" Joe said, surprised that Ms. Ziebarth hadn't mentioned it.

"That's what people at the university said. After their argument, Klingner banned her from his lab. But several witnesses saw her there again." Riley paused. "On the morning Klingner was killed."

"Do you know who the witnesses are?" Joe asked.

"A Professor Holt; one of Holt's graduate assistants, Tang Ly Koo; and the department secretary, Rhonda Barnes." Con checked his wristwatch. "Listen, fellas, I can't say any more. Why don't you go talk to Ziebarth. She was bailed out last night and is probably at home."

Frank and Joe thanked Officer Riley, looked up Yvonne Ziebarth's address, and headed in that direction.

Ziebarth's apartment building was a clean, ten-story brick building occupying most of a block in a quiet residential section of Bayport. As the brothers climbed out of the van, Frank was shaking his head.

"Joe, I'm not so sure about Ms. Ziebarth," he said. "Why didn't she tell you she was banned from the lab? And if she was banned, why was she in his lab the day he was murdered?"

"Come on, let's go," Joe said. "We're not going to find any answers standing around out here."

The Hardys went into the vestibule, buzzed

Ziebarth's apartment, waited and buzzed again, but got no answer.

"I'd hate to leave after coming this far," Frank said. "How nimble do your fingers feel?"

Joe grinned and slipped a set of small tools resembling dental probes out from his wallet. He worked them into the lock as Frank shielded what Joe was doing with his body. A few moments later a click sounded. Joe pushed open the door and they slipped inside.

Upstairs at the apartment door, they knocked, but there was no answer. On a whim, Joe tried the doorknob. It turned. The brothers cautiously edged the door open.

"Ms. Ziebarth?" Joe called.

Stepping inside, they saw a futon couch, a small Oriental rug, a brass floor lamp, and two healthy looking spider plants hanging in the window. There was a white desk by the window with a computer and printer.

"Nice place," said Frank.

Just then a deep voice boomed out from the doorway behind them: "All right, freeze! Put your hands behind your head, then turn around slowly. Easy does it or I blow your brains out."

# Chapter

## 3

JOE TENSED FOR ACTION. He was ready to spin and face their opponent, but he resisted the impulse and did as he was told. The first thing he saw was the barrel of a black 9-millimeter automatic pistol pointed directly at his head.

Joe raised his eyes from the gun and found himself looking into the same unsmiling face he'd seen in the school parking lot the day before. Detective Henry Broussard lowered his pistol and walked past them into the apartment, glowering.

"I should have known I'd run into you again," the big man growled, shaking his head. He slipped his automatic back inside his jacket, then shrugged to seat it comfortably in its shoulder holster. "Yvonne Ziebarth told me she lives alone. What're you two doing here?"

"We came to talk with her," Frank said.

"Uh-huh. And how, exactly, did you get in?"

"The door was unlocked," Joe said.

"Does she always leave it unlocked?" Broussard asked suspiciously.

"We don't know," Joe said. "We've never been here."

"And what did you come to talk to her about?"

Joe met the detective's eyes. "About the trouble she's in," he said. "We're just here to try to help a friend."

"I've heard you two have quite a reputation for meddling in police business," the detective said. "But let's get one thing clear from the start—this will not happen while I'm in charge of this case. Understood?"

"Yes, sir," Frank said, trying to ease the tension. "Understood."

Joe faced the detective. "If it's not too confidential, Detective Broussard," he said, "were you following us or did you come here to talk to Ms. Ziebarth, too?"

Broussard stared at Joe and his eyes narrowed. Then he said, "You know that's none of your business. But it just so happens Ms. Ziebarth was supposed to come to the station to answer some questions this morning. She never showed up. Since you two are such good friends of hers, maybe you can tell me where she went."

"I'm afraid I don't know, sir," Frank said, sticking to the polite approach.

"I'm afraid I don't either," Joe said. Then he turned to his brother. "Frank, this doesn't sound good. Her ex-boss has been killed. Now she's missing, And her door was left open. Maybe something—"

"Most likely she just made a run for it," Broussard interrupted. "They do it all the time." He plucked a piece of lint from his jacket sleeve and flicked it aside. "We'll catch her, though. You can count on that."

"I don't believe she'd run," said Joe.

"Well, if she so much as crossed Bayport city limits, she's in big trouble," Broussard said. "One condition of her bail was to stay in town. If we find her somewhere else, she's going back to jail and she won't be getting out this time. You be sure to pass that along to her if you see her. I'm headed back to my office now. And don't forget, fellas—I don't need any teenage amateurs telling me how to do my job. So stay out of my investigation."

With that Broussard stepped to one side of the door and extended his arm, showing Frank and Joe the way out.

"What do you think?" Joe said, as they climbed into the van.

"About her not being there?" Frank asked.

Joe nodded. "She could be in real trouble."

"Joe, maybe you just don't want to think she took off because you don't want her to be guilty," Frank said, and put the key in the ignition.

"I don't know what to think. I guess we start looking for clues."

"Good choice," Frank said, starting the engine. Shifting into gear, he said, "Next stop: Bayport University!"

The university campus featured rolling hills, tree-lined drives, and old brick buildings with tall white columns and ivy clinging to their walls. It was a small university, but its reputation was strong in the sciences. Many of its graduates went on to medical school or advanced research. The science center was a large three-story yellow-brick building with a circular driveway and a large parking lot. It appeared to be new and well maintained.

The Hardys stopped for directions from a group of students—most of whom wore cut-off jeans, T-shirts, and sandals and had bright nylon book bags slung over their shoulders.

"Did you ever notice how high school kids wear T-shirts with the names of colleges," Joe said, "but college kids only wear T-shirts with the names of high schools?"

Frank smiled. "Attaboy, Joe. Keep those

powers of observation sharp and we'll crack this case before you know it."

Inside the building they found a map that showed the chemistry department was on the second floor. Upstairs, a silver-haired woman sat talking on a telephone. Her glasses rode low on the tip of her nose, and she politely held up a finger for them to wait until she finished her phone call. The nameplate on her desk read Mrs. Rhonda Barnes—Department Secretary. Con Riley had mentioned her as one of the witnesses who placed Yvonne Ziebarth at the lab the day of Dr. Klingner's death.

"Yes, I believe Dr. Holt just got out of class," Mrs. Barnes said. "Hold, please, and I'll connect you." She pressed a button, then hung up and smiled at the Hardys.

"You're here for pass/no-credit forms, right? We always have a big rush just before the deadline." She began reaching into a drawer.

"Uh, no, ma'am," Frank said. "Actually, we're not students here. We've come about Professor Klingner."

"Oh. We were all so sorry. It was such a shock."

At that moment a middle-aged man of medium height and build, wearing an open white lab coat over blue jeans, a checked button-down shirt, and a bright green bow tie, hurried past the desk and over to a bank of open mailboxes. He pulled envelopes and brochures from one and turned to leave.

"Excuse me a moment," Mrs. Barnes said to the Hardys. "Dr. Holt, I just transferred a call to your office. It was Professor Brooke."

"Thanks, Rhonda. I'll call him from the lab."

"Sir?" Joe said, taking a step toward the professor. "Could I take a minute of your time to ask a quick question or two?"

Holt eyed the brothers. "How can I help you? Do you need a signature for one of my classes?" Holt wore silver wire-framed glasses beneath a mane of gray hair.

"It's nothing like that, sir," Joe said. "I'm Joe Hardy, and this is my brother, Frank. We're looking into Dr. Klingner's death."

The professor grew serious. "You seem young for investigative work."

"We work with our father a lot," Frank said. "He's a well-known PI in the area."

Holt shook his head somberly. "It was a shock, I can tell you that." He paused. "I'd like to answer your questions but I've got an awfully busy day ahead."

"Just a couple of quick ones," Joe said. "Do you know Yvonne Ziebarth?"

"Of course. She was Klingner's graduate assistant."

"We understand you saw them argue," Joe continued.

"That's right. Several of us did. It was quite a scene."

"And this happened when?" Joe said.

Holt slid back the sleeve of his lab coat and looked at his watch. "Listen, fellas, let's not stand out here talking. Come on to my office. I can give you a quick few minutes, but that's it."

"Thanks, Dr. Holt," Joe said. They followed the professor to his office. It was a medium-size room with a large wooden desk and chairs, walls lined with books, and a colorful three-dimensional model of a complex molecule perched atop a large filing cabinet. Holt settled behind the desk and gestured for the brothers to take the chairs in front.

"All right, Mr."—he paused—"Hardy, is it?"

"Yes, sir," Joe said.

"You wanted to know when I saw Yvonne Ziebarth and Dr. Klingner arguing. Let's see. It was a big blowup. I don't remember the exact date, but Klingner banned Ziebarth from the lab. Then she showed up the other day— the day Klingner died, actually. By the way, I've already given all this information to the police."

"Do you know what the argument was about?" Joe continued.

"Something to do with experiments, but I couldn't tell you what exactly."

28

At that moment a tall, thin young man appeared at the open door. He was also wearing a white lab coat. He was carrying a tray of calibrated flasks and stainless steel beakers.

"Dr. Holt," he said, bowing ever so slightly, and sounding apologetic about interrupting. "The new supplies have arrived. You asked me to let you know." The young man turned to leave.

"Tang, wait a moment," Holt said. "Frank and Joe Hardy, this is Tang Ly Koo, one of my two graduate student assistants." There were polite nods all around and Holt continued. "Tang, you saw Yvonne Ziebarth here the other day. What did you tell the police? Any idea why she was here?"

"Sorry, but I do not know anything," he said, shrugging at the brothers. "I did not know the police wanted to speak with me."

Dr. Holt thanked Koo, and the grad assistant went back to work.

"Well, I'll tell you everything *I* know," Holt said. "It's not much, and I'm not clear on all the details. Klingner was in biochemistry, which isn't my field. I'm an organic chemist. My specialty is noncarbon compounds, especially metals. Right now I'm researching chemical reactions involving electricity." Holt caught himself and smiled. "But you don't want to know about my work, you want to know about Dr. Klingner's, don't you? It had something to do with energy transfer at the cellular level. Ms. Ziebarth was very closely involved." With that Professor Holt glanced down at his watch again. "Now I'm afraid I've really got to run to a meeting, so if you'll excuse me . . ."

The Hardys thanked Dr. Holt and watched the busy professor rush off with notebook in hand and coattails flying.

"What do you think, Frank?" Joe asked as they walked back to the reception area. "Is there anyone else we should talk to while we're here?"

Mrs. Barnes obviously overheard Joe's question and said, "Well, you might try Dr. Holt's other graduate student assistant, Marcus Stevens. He was here just a moment ago. He should be right back. Oh, here he is now."

The Hardys turned to face Marcus Stevens. He was a surprising contrast to the tall, dignified Tang. Stevens appeared to be barely out of junior high school. His plumpness bordered on baby fat. His skin was deathly pale, no doubt from spending all his time under fluorescent lights. He wore thick-lensed, black-framed glasses, dark pants high on his waist, and a white short-sleeved shirt with a white T-shirt underneath. His petulant frown made him resemble a three-year-old ready to throw a tantrum at any moment.

"You're a graduate student?" Joe said.

Frank cringed, thinking, Joe! Will you ever learn any tact?

Stevens's eyes flashed. If he had a sore spot, Joe had just jabbed it.

"If it's any of your business," Stevens replied dryly, "yes, I am. You probably think I look young. For your information I am seventeen years old and a Ph.D. candidate."

They couldn't help but notice his tone of superiority. He turned and walked down the corridor away from them. The Hardys followed.

Frank cleared his throat. "Okay, to get to the reason we're here—ah, can I call you Marc?"

"I prefer Marcus," Stevens said, turning to face them again.

Joe didn't like the guy one bit. He was the same age as Joe, but he obviously thought he was hot stuff just because he was in a doctoral program.

"Marcus," Frank said, "the reason we're here is that yesterday Yvonne Ziebarth was arrested for the murder of Dr. Thomas Klingner and we're looking into it."

"You're not with the police, though, are you?" Stevens said.

"Not exactly," Frank said.

"I didn't think so," Stevens said. "In that case I have nothing to say to you, and as far as I'm concerned, this conversation's over. I've got work to do."

"Well, so do we," Joe said, taking a step toward Stevens.

Frank gripped his brothers' arm.

"Fine," Frank said to Stevens. "Thanks for your time, and if anything comes to mind, will you give us a call?" Frank scribbled his name and number on a piece of paper. He handed it to Stevens, who took it without looking at it and dropped it into his lab coat pocket. Then Stevens turned and walked away without another word.

"Man, what's *his* problem?" Joe said.

"Maybe he's overworked," Frank said. "Or maybe he thought someone insulted him."

"Or maybe," Joe said, "he knows something he doesn't want to tell.

"Let's go take a look around Klingner's lab," Joe said, keeping his voice down so as not to be overheard again.

"But the cops have already been through it."

"Frank," Joe said, "you and I both know if we take our time we're bound to come up with something new. Come on."

They headed farther down the corridor to a door with yellow plastic tape with black lettering that read Crime Scene—Do Not Enter stretched across it. The brothers approached the door and exchanged a look. Joe carefully lifted the tape, turned the door handle, and walked in.

The lab was a large room with exposed pipes, ducts, and ventilation shafts running overhead like a maze.

"Looks pretty makeshift for a high-tech lab," Frank observed.

"Actually, it's built that way on purpose," Joe explained. "They don't want all that stuff hidden behind walls. If they need more electrical wiring or water lines or waste removal, they just add it right on top."

"Is that another one of those brilliant insights you picked up in Ms. Ziebarth's class?" Frank asked.

"Whatever," Joe responded.

The room was filled with refrigerators, deep sinks, and shelves with test-tube racks and brown glass bottles on them.

Joe walked to a row of gallon-size red metal cans with screw-on lids. "Safety cans," he said, pointing to one. "You store dangerous chemicals in them."

Above one sink was a huge wooden Peg-Board with pencil-size wooden dowels sticking out. Test tubes, flasks, and beakers were hung on the dowels to dry. Next to the sinks were small cardboard boxes that dispensed different-colored rubber gloves—blue, yellow, and green—one at a time, like tissues. They could hear the soft hum of a pump, which was attached to a vacuum oven for drying out samples of solids.

They looked around for a few minutes. Finally, Frank said, "Now, what do you guess this is for?"

Near the door was a shiny metal sphere the size of a soccer ball suspended by a long chain attached to the ceiling. It was held against the wall by a metal hook.

"Looks like a pendulum," Joe said. "Maybe to study conservation of energy. See? They let it swing across the lab bench over there and measure its speed."

"That sounds more like physics than chemistry," Frank said.

"True, but maybe this room doubles for both," Joe said, and continued to search.

There was a side door from the lab leading to an attached office. They went in. "That must be where Ms. Ziebarth worked," Joe said.

Frank noticed a desk clock beside the computer. He checked it against the time on his watch and said, "Joe, I just remembered. I'm supposed to call Callie.

"I'll go make a quick call from the van. Be right back." There was a phone in the office, but Frank knew better than to risk leaving his fingerprints at a crime scene.

"I'll keep looking around," Joe said, and kept up his methodical search. Nothing stood out. He knew sometimes it helped to change his point of view. He climbed onto one of the tables and peered down at the room. Nothing from up there. Next he got down on his hands and knees and crawled around. Sure enough, under one of the lab benches beside a trash can he spotted a small, crumpled-up piece of paper. It was white and shiny.

Carefully, Joe picked up the piece of paper. He held it by one corner so as not to smudge any fingerprints. It was roughly the size of a grape. It wasn't ordinary paper, but slick. He had been examining the little ball for several minutes when he heard a soft, metallic click behind him. It came from near the door.

Joe turned and in an instant recognized the metal pendulum sphere, unmoored from its hook, swinging smoothly through the air in a direct line for his head.

# Chapter

## 4

JOE JERKED HIS HEAD sideways. Normally, his quick reflexes would have saved him, but the heavy sphere had swung too far in its silent arc. It struck him a glancing blow—enough to send an explosion of light flashing through his brain and to bring the ground rushing up to him.

Joe next felt the cool tile floor against his cheek and heard a loud thumping inside his head. He realized it was his heartbeat. He heard a pair of shoes stepping close beside his head. He was struggling to regain his senses. The footsteps paused—he couldn't tell for how long—then clicked away across the floor. A few moments later he heard the echo of a stairwell door slamming.

Joe managed to push himself up, woozy and blinking down at the floor. Another few seconds and he stumbled to his feet. The crumpled piece of paper was gone. His attacker had taken it.

Joe staggered to the window on rubbery legs. He saw a small, red sedan back quickly out of a space in the parking lot directly below and dart toward an exit. The car had to stop for traffic. Joe could sense the driver's impatience as whoever it was waited for an opening. Finally the car moved into the stream of cars, forcing one yellow pickup to swerve sharply and blast its horn.

Joe searched the parking lot quickly and spotted the familiar black van.

"Frank!" Joe shouted at the glass, but his brother couldn't hear him. He could see Frank through the windshield, sitting in the driver's seat, holding the cellular phone to his ear. Joe fumbled at the metal frame for the latch, but the windows were new, double-paned, energy-efficient models that didn't open.

"Frank!" Joe yelled again, and thumped the thick, insulated glass with his palms. All he could do was watch the red car make a sharp left onto the avenue. He squinted but couldn't make out the license plate as the car sped away. He left the lab, making sure not to disturb the crime scene tape on his way out the door. He went down the back stairs skirting the reception area and out to the van.

On their way home, Joe told Frank all about the attack in the lab. "We should follow up as soon as possible," Joe said. "That piece of paper must have been pretty important. Somebody almost killed me to get it."

"Who knows?" Frank speculated. "Maybe whoever it was just stumbled on you snooping around the lab. If you hadn't found the paper, they might never have known it was there. . . ."

The next day after school Frank and Joe headed straight back to Bayport University. Since their only lead was the red car, they had decided to stake out the parking lot at the science building.

"You'd recognize the car, wouldn't you?" Frank asked, pulling their van into the lot.

"I was groggy from that whack on the head, but I think so," Joe said. They nosed into a slot in the middle of the lot with good views in both directions.

After almost an hour of sitting in the van, the brothers began to feel the effects of the late-spring afternoon sun. Joe caught himself dozing off.

"I'm roasting," Frank said.

"Me, too," Joe said with a yawn. "How about if I go inside and get us a cold drink?"

He remembered there was a soda machine just inside the side entrance.

"Great idea," Frank said. "I'll keep watch."

As Joe went over to the building, the cellular phone in the van rang. Frank picked up. It was his girlfriend, Callie Shaw. "I was just thinking about you," Frank said.

As he started to chat, Frank saw Joe push open the door of the building with one hand while balancing two cans of soda in the other. Out of the corner of his eye, Frank also saw a red car pull into the parking lot. It started down the aisle toward where Joe was walking. The driver must have seen Joe watching him the day before because the car made a quick U-turn and, with a screech of tires, headed out of the parking lot.

When he heard the screech, Joe looked up. Frank said, "Sorry, Callie, got to go." He hung up, then yelled, "Hurry up, Joe, he's getting away!" Joe sprinted to the van, dropping the sodas as he ran. Frank leaned out of his window but couldn't see the car's license plate number. He did watch it turn left as it exited the lot, though.

Frank had the engine gunned so they could take off as soon as Joe got in. Glancing both ways at the exit, Frank found an opening in traffic and made a quick left. They were headed directly into the sun and both brothers squinted at the glare.

"I couldn't see who it was, just that he—"

" 'He'?" Frank interrupted. "It was a he?"

"Or she," Joe said. "I'm not sure."

Frank threaded his way through a steady stream of cars. "Do you see him?" he asked.

Joe was leaning forward in his seat as far as his seat belt would allow, his hands on the dashboard. "Not yet. . . . No . . . Wait . . . There.

"In front of the station wagon, passing the truck."

Frank saw a compact red sedan darting ahead.

"You're sure it's the one from yesterday?" Frank kept his eyes trained on the small sedan.

"Almost a hundred percent sure," Joe said.

"Okay, let's see where he's going," Frank said.

The Hardys stayed about six car lengths back, close enough to keep their prey in sight. Traffic conditions weren't bad for surveillance: light enough so that not many vehicles crowded in in front of them, yet heavy enough to keep the black van from standing out.

"He's heading for the parkway," Joe said. His eyes flicked to the gas gauge, where the needle hovered near the big red *E*. "Uh-oh, I meant to fill up last night, but with all the excitement . . . Maybe we should try to pull him over."

"Negative," said Frank. "If he tried to take

off with so many cars around, somebody might get hurt. Let's just stay with him and hope he turns off soon."

They followed the red compact through the outskirts of Bayport and across the city line. Soon after, there was a sign that said Greenfield—1 Mile.

"I wish his license plate wasn't so dirty so I could make it out," said Joe.

Frank sped up gradually, passed several cars, and came within three car lengths of their suspect. They were both straining to read the plate number when the red car abruptly swerved into the Exit Only lane.

"You think he spotted us?" Joe asked.

"Don't know," Frank shot back.

The small red car followed the long, sweeping arc of the exit ramp, slowed at the Stop sign, then turned left. Frank followed as closely as he dared. Downtown Greenfield had medium-size apartment buildings, a supermarket, a video rental store, a pizza shop, a record store, and a few other small shops.

Another two blocks and the red car turned right. As they cruised past a gas station, Frank said, "Too bad we don't have time to stop."

The sedan's brake lights went on as it took a sharp left down the ramp of an underground parking garage. By the time the Hardys pulled up, the car had disappeared behind a sliding metal door.

"Terrific," Joe said. "We come all this way and still don't know who the driver is."

"At least we know he—or she—is in that building. Let's go check it out," Frank said.

"Now, there's one that rings a bell." Frank was pointing to a nameplate on the front door buzzers.

" 'M. Stevens.' I bet it's that nerd Stevens," Joe said. "Apartment Three-G. Maybe I can get him to tell me what he did with that wad of paper he whacked me for."

"If it was evidence that could be used against him," Frank said, "he's probably destroyed it."

"If he hasn't destroyed the evidence, let's not give him a chance to," Joe said.

"The problem is," Frank said, "if we buzz up, we lose the element of surprise."

Joe reached past his brother and pressed his right palm across all the buttons above Stevens's nameplate.

"What are you doing?" Frank said.

A moment later a half-dozen different voices sounded through the round metal intercom speaker..

"Who is it?" . . . "Yes?" . . . "Who's there?"

Joe leaned close to the speaker. "Western Union with a telegram."

There was a pause and one voice said, "Are you sure you've got the right apartment?"

Then there was another pause, and the buzzer sounded.

Joe grinned as he yanked open the door. "There's always at least one sucker for a telegram."

Above the lobby elevator was a dial that was just revolving to a halt on three.

"Three-G, right?" Joe said. "Come on, let's take the stairs. Maybe we can cut him off before he gets inside the apartment."

They took the stairs two at a time. At the third floor landing, Joe held up a hand and cautiously opened the door. When its metal hinges creaked, Joe grimaced and pushed the door open wide. In the dim light of the hallway, he found himself staring into the face of Marcus Stevens.

Stevens was fitting his key into his apartment door. He turned and stared at Frank and Joe in surprise for a couple of seconds. Then his face froze in a frown, and he snarled, "What are you two doing here? Did you follow me?"

"Just settle down, Stevens," Joe countered, stepping from the stairwell with Frank at his heels. "We've got some questions for you."

"Is that right?" Stevens muttered.

"That's right," Joe said. "About the university and Klingner's lab. And about your whacking me over the head yesterday and stealing a certain piece of crumpled-up paper that was in my hand."

"I have no idea what you're talking about," Stevens said. "And if you continue to harass me, I'm going to call the police."

Joe took a step toward the belligerent graduate student. "You listen to me, my friend," he said. "There's been one murder and one serious assault so far. Yvonne Ziebarth is missing, and if anything has happened to her—"

At that moment a latch clicked and the door to Stevens's apartment was opened from the inside.

Standing in the doorway, her face paler than usual, was Yvonne Ziebarth.

# Chapter
## 5

FOR A MOMENT they just stood there staring at one another. Ms. Ziebarth seemed to be as surprised to see the Hardys as they were to see her.

Finally Joe broke the silence. "Ms. Ziebarth, what are you doing here?"

"Hello, Joe. Hello, Frank," she said. "I . . . er. Why don't you come in?" Ms. Ziebarth said and turned to Stevens. "If that's all right with you, Marcus."

Stevens shrugged. "Sure, Yvonne. Whatever you want."

The apartment was small and furnished modestly. There was a sagging sofa, two mismatched armchairs, a stained coffee table, and faded throw rugs in the living room. Makeshift bookshelves were crammed with thick science textbooks, scholarly journals, and a huge number of science-fiction paperbacks.

Science fiction, typical for a science nerd like Stevens, Joe thought. He probably spent hours reading.

"Have a seat, guys," Ziebarth said. "Can I get you a soda?"

Frank and Joe nodded gratefully. Stevens followed Ziebarth into the little kitchen nook to help her with glasses and ice. A few moments later, the four of them settled back in the living room.

"First, you should know Marcus and I are good friends," Ziebarth said. "We saw each other constantly at the department, and I consider him a valuable colleague."

Joe glanced at Stevens and spotted what he thought was a flicker of disappointment in his eyes. Ms. Ziebarth might consider them just friends, Joe thought, but he obviously wished it was more.

"And I turned to him in my time of need," Ziebarth continued. "You two may be used to dealing with murder and mayhem, but I'm a scientist. Give me my lab coat, a computer, some data to analyze, and I'm happy. So when someone I know is killed and the police arrest me ..." She glanced into her glass and swished the ice cubes around. "I was on my way to see Detective Broussard this morning and panicked. I drove past my exit and came straight here. I'm glad Marcus was home."

Joe thought he saw Stevens's face light up.

"Anyway, I know skipping the appointment with the detective was probably the worst thing I could have done," Ziebarth said, "but I was scared."

"Well, Broussard is definitely after you now," Frank said.

"We ran into him at your apartment yesterday when we went there to talk to you," Joe explained. "He thinks you're on the run."

"We were pretty surprised your apartment door was unlocked," said Frank, changing the subject a bit.

"Unlocked?" Ziebarth said. "That just proves what a mess I've been. I haven't once forgotten to lock that door in six years."

"Ms. Ziebarth," Joe said, "I think we can help you, but you're going to have to come clean with us about a few things."

"Such as your big argument with Klingner," Frank said. "And his banning you from the lab."

Ziebarth paused and said, "You know all about that?"

"We spoke to some people at the university," Joe said.

"I didn't want to bring any of this up," Ziebarth said. "But I guess the truth's important now. Yes, Dr. Klingner and I did have an argument. You see, he broke one of the most sacred commandments of academia. He refused to give credit where credit was due." She paused a moment. "Dr. Klingner stole my research."

"How did he do that?" Joe asked.

"I was conducting some experiments entirely on my own," she said. "And I came up with results not even Dr. Klingner could have foreseen.

"When I showed him my findings, I expected him to congratulate me and contact the editors of some of the top scientific journals." She shook her head. "Dr. Klingner telephoned the editors, all right—to claim *he'd* come up with the findings!"

"What did these experiments involve?" Frank asked.

"The citrus acid cycle. It's a fundamental source of energy in all plant and animal cellular activity." Catching the Hardys' puzzled looks, Ziebarth added, "You'd need about a dozen advanced chem courses to appreciate the fine points."

Stevens sniffed and said, "Most of the material is far beyond the high-school level."

"Why didn't you turn Klingner in?" Joe said, ignoring Stevens's nasty dig. "You could have taken your case to the department chairperson."

Ziebarth shook her head. "Klingner would

have denied it. It would have been my word against his. In a battle like that, guess who wins? He's older, more established, a professor. I'm just a lowly grad student. People would have accused me of trying to steal *his* work.

"Anyway, after our blowup, Klingner told me never to set foot in the lab again." She shrugged. "That's when I took the teaching job at Bayport High."

"But despite being banned," Frank said, "you did visit again—on the day Klingner died, right?"

Ziebarth sighed. "I got a message from Dr. Klingner asking me to come to the lab that morning. I thought he might have reconsidered. Maybe he wanted to apologize. So I went."

"And?" Frank prompted.

"And nothing. I got there and waited. I waited some more, but he never showed up. I finally left."

"That's when Professor Holt, Tang Ly Koo, and Rhonda Barnes saw you?" Joe asked.

Ziebarth nodded as she leaned forward to press her point home. "I don't deny I was there, but I never saw Dr. Klingner. And I certainly didn't switch the label on that phosgene canister."

"After you left the department that day, where did you go?" Frank asked.

"Just a minute," said Stevens, standing up and hooking his thumbs into the black suspenders he was wearing in place of a belt. "I think that's enough. There's no reason for you two to put her through this."

"We're not putting her through anything the police and the district attorney won't," Frank said. "Only they won't be so polite."

"It's okay, Marcus," Ziebarth said.

"Let's go back to the poisoning itself," Frank continued. "I picture Klingner working in his lab. There's a tank labeled Oxygen ..."

Ziebarth nodded. "He was experimenting to see the effects of various gases on bacteria."

"He opens the oxygen canister," Frank went on, "only the label is phony and the thing is full of phosgene."

"Phosgene has a very distinctive smell," Joe said. "Like newly mown grass."

"Good, Joe," Ziebarth said, lapsing into her role as chemistry teacher for the first time that afternoon. "I can see you've been doing your research."

"Klingner must have known about the smell," Joe said. "Why didn't he just leave as soon as he recognized it?"

"He probably didn't have time," Stevens said. "Phosgene is very powerful. Even a small amount can kill a human being very quickly." His words echoed in the room for a moment, as if the thought of such a deadly poison had shocked them into silence.

Finally Ziebarth looked at the Hardys and said, "I've got a question for you two. What brought you here?"

Joe looked sharply at Stevens. "Maybe Marcus can answer that."

"I—I certainly can," Stevens sputtered. "They followed me home."

"Followed you after you tried to kill me yesterday," Joe shot back.

Ziebarth turned to Stevens. "Is that true?"

"I wasn't trying to hurt him." Stevens shrugged. "Just scare him off."

"Some way to scare me off," Joe said. "A direct hit with that pendulum and I would be dead."

"You threw something at him?" Ziebarth asked, dumbfounded. "Why?"

"Because I found something in the lab," Joe continued. "A piece of evidence he didn't want anyone else to see."

"Marcus, what is it?" Ziebarth asked.

Stevens got up and went into his bedroom. When he returned, he placed a piece of paper on the coffee table.

"I uncrumpled it," he mumbled. "It's blank."

"But, Marcus," said Ziebarth, "why did you think you had to steal it?"

"I could tell it was important by the way Joe

was studying it. I figured they were building a case and it would be used as evidence against you." He shrugged. "I took it to protect you, Yvonne."

"But, Marcus, any evidence they find can only help me because I didn't kill Dr. Klingner."

"Maybe it's time we examined that piece of evidence," Frank suggested.

Stevens reached for it.

"Wait," Joe said, flashing his impatience, "there might be fingerprints if you haven't smudged them all yet."

Frank stood up and went over to the kitchen counter where there was a glass jar full of chopsticks. He chose two.

A minute later Frank had turned the paper over twice.

"It looks like the backing on a label," Joe said. "The shiny part you peel off before you stick the label on something."

"If it's from the oxygen label on the phosgene tank," Frank said. "It could lead us straight to Klingner's killer."

"But how did it get where Joe found it?" Ziebarth asked.

"Easy," Frank said. "The killer typed the phony label, peeled off the backing, balled it up, and tossed it toward the trash can, not noticing that it didn't go in."

"That seems pretty careless," Ziebarth said.

"We've seen a lot worse," Joe said.

"I bet it won't have any fingerprints at all," Stevens said. "Why don't I just take it with me and check it tomorrow on one of the microscopes at the department?" He reached out, but Joe's hand clamped down on his pale wrist before he could grab the paper.

"We'll take care of it, Marcus," Joe said firmly.

"You know that by being here you're violating your bail?" Frank said to Ziebarth. "The police could throw you right back in jail."

"Stop trying to scare her!" Stevens said. "Don't trust these guys, Yvonne. They don't care about you, all they want to do is take credit for solving this murder."

Ziebarth shook her head. "You're wrong, Marcus. I do trust them."

"If there's anyone she shouldn't trust," Joe said, facing Stevens, "it's you."

Just then there was a loud knock at the door. "Police!" came a deep, familiar-sounding voice.

Stevens froze.

"Better open it," Frank said.

Stevens turned to Ziebarth. "Quick, go in the other room," he said. Ziebarth hesitated. There were four more knocks on the door, and the voice boomed, "I said police. Open up!"

Ziebarth glanced at Joe, rose uncertainly, and headed for the bedroom, closing the door softly behind her. Stevens said, "Coming." He went to the front door and opened it.

Detective Broussard barged in past Stevens and stood in the middle of the room. "Frank and Joe Hardy again," he said. "I noticed your van outside. I remember yesterday you agreed to stay out of the Klingner murder investigation, so I'll assume this is just coincidence meeting you here."

The detective turned to Stevens. "Yvonne Ziebarth was supposed to meet me at the precinct this morning, but she never showed. Any idea where she might be?"

"Well, ahh . . ."

Broussard squinted. "Careful, Stevens. This is a murder investigation."

Broussard glanced at the closed door to the bedroom, then at the table. "And before you tell me you haven't seen her, let me make a few observations. First of all, there are three of you in this room, but I count four glasses on the table."

Stevens opened his mouth to say something, but Broussard held up a hand to quiet him. The Hardys could both see that the detective was in fine form.

"And don't tell me you had a friend here who left because the ice in those drinks hasn't melted yet. I just walked in here, but you don't know how long I've been standing outside in the hallway, do you?"

Broussard pulled back the bottom of his sport coat and rested one hand on a pair of handcuffs that was clipped to his belt. He leaned in close to Stevens and said, "Don't lie to me, son. Because if you do, your friend Ms. Ziebarth won't be the only one I arrest."

"Just a minute," came a voice from the bedroom as the door swung open to reveal Yvonne Ziebarth. "He was only trying to help me."

"Young lady," Broussard said, "you were already in a lot of trouble. But by skipping our meeting this morning and leaving town, you just made things worse."

"I'm sorry," she said. "I was just scared and panicked."

"Excuse me, sir," Joe said, "but all she did wrong was come here. She admits her mistake. You don't have to rearrest her, do you?"

Broussard slipped his hands in his pockets and rocked back on his heels. He took his time answering.

"All right," he said. "No arrest. But we're going down to the station house now. You're going to answer some questions, and you're going to stay in touch. Otherwise, I lock you up—without bail this time."

Ziebarth thanked the detective, said goodbye to Marcus Stevens and the Hardys, and followed the officer out to his car.

The Hardys left moments later. In a voice

that was equal parts salutation and threat, Joe said, "We'll be in touch, Marcus. You're off the hook for now, but we'll be watching you." Stevens slammed the door behind them after they left.

On their way home, the Hardys mulled over the case. Their only solid clue so far was the label backing. They decided to analyze it the next day at school, then go back to the university in the afternoon and try to develop more leads.

"I feel like this case is just getting started," Joe said. "We may have a few surprises ahead."

Frank and Joe were discussing the case again as they pulled into the high school parking lot very late the next morning. They both collected their books, got out, and started running toward the school to beat the late bell.

Hearing a car engine whine at high RPMs, they turned and saw a small red car almost on top of them.

The next few seconds were a blur.

Joe saw the driver pitch a cylindrical object out of his window that sailed toward them in a neat arc. There was the sound of metal clanging on pavement, and Joe realized it was a length of pipe. A thick cloud of dark gray smoke billowed out of the pipe, and before Joe knew it, he and his brother were bent over, coughing, choking, and rubbing their eyes.

Joe heard the engine wind down and wind up again as if it were changing direction. Then the engine roared and started to get loud again very fast.

"Watch it, Frank," Joe shouted. "He's coming back at us!"

# Chapter

# 6

JOE SHOVED HIS BROTHER out of the car's path, sending him sprawling. Frank's backpack flew off his shoulder, and his books tumbled out.

Joe heard the engine roar loud in his ears as he tried to turn his head to catch a glimpse of the driver. But the smoke was too thick, and things were happening too fast. All he could see, before the left front fender hit his sneaker with a hollow thump, was a silhouette at the wheel.

The impact on his shoe was enough to send him sprawling. He came down hard, and the rough asphalt stung his palms.

Joe jumped to his feet and raced over to his brother. Frank was getting up slowly, a long rip down the side of his jeans. There was a black tire mark across his book bag.

"Frank, are you all right?"

"Yep, but that was too close," Frank said, squinting through the swirling cloud of smoke.

"Come on," Joe said. "Let's get him."

They ran back to the van and jumped in, but Frank said, "Forget it. By time we get out of here, he'll be five miles ahead. Did you see him?"

Joe shook his head. "Not the driver, not the license plate. It sure looked like Stevens's car, though. What do you say we head over to the university and talk to him? He's bound to show up there eventually."

"I think we're better off going to class right now, Joe."

"All right, we'll catch up to Super-Nerd later," Joe said.

Frank patted his shirt pocket where he had the label backing safely stashed in a small envelope. "We can check out our one big piece of evidence in the lab and see if we can lift fingerprints from it," he said as three teachers descended on them.

The boys had to explain to the teachers that the smoke bomb was just a prank. Better that than involve the police, in which case they could have been tied up for an hour making a statement.

\* \* \*

Frank and Joe met Callie and Vanessa for lunch in the school cafeteria. They brought the girls up to date on the case so far.

"Did you find any fingerprints?" Callie asked.

"Not a single one," Frank said. "The label's too crumpled."

"Wait a second," Callie interjected. "We can assume the killer did touch that label. So why don't we analyze it chemically? The person may have had traces of chemicals on their fingers. Maybe a tiny amount was left on the label."

"If we're lucky," Vanessa continued, "we could trace that chemical back to a particular lab or experiment."

"It might not hold up in court," Frank said, "but it might be a good lead. Do you think we could detect the small amount that might have rubbed off someone's fingers?"

"We can with the new PIXE machine," Vanessa said. She went on to explain that the machine was part of the equipment in a "floating lab" program where sophisticated and expensive instruments were lent to schools for a few weeks so students could learn about them. "PIXE is Photon Induced X-ray Emission. PIXE, for short," Vanessa explained. "I'm not sure exactly how it works, but I know it bombards objects with photons that emit X rays. Since different elements give off electrons in different ways, a PIXE analysis can identify even the tiniest amount of a substance."

"Sounds like a great idea," Joe said.

"Do you know how to work the machine?" asked Frank.

"Absolutely," Callie said at the exact same time as Vanessa said, "Not really." They both laughed, and Callie said, "What we don't know, we can figure out."

Frank handed Callie the little envelope containing the label backing and said, "It's all yours. Good luck."

"Here's hoping your advanced placement chemistry pays off," Joe added.

After school that afternoon Frank and Joe drove to the university. On the way over Frank asked Joe if he'd heard anything about Ms. Ziebarth.

"Broussard let her go after questioning her yesterday. I called her at home between classes. She was with her lawyer. She said she was going to take at least a few days off."

"That makes sense," Frank said. "She'll need to rest up. Did she say anything more about the case?"

"Nope," Joe said.

As they got out of the van and strode toward the entrance of the Bayport U. science building, Joe said, "I've been looking forward to our little date with Super-Nerd all day."

They took the back stairs to the third floor

and found Marcus Stevens in Professor Holt's lab sitting at a bench writing on a clipboard.

The grad student looked up and scowled. "Great, it's the Hardy boys," he said, "everybody's favorite teenage detectives. Do you have a real reason to be here or is it just to harass me more?"

"We were wondering where you were between eight fifty-five and nine-ten this morning," Frank said.

Stevens frowned. "What do you care?" he asked.

"For your information," Joe said, "somebody driving a car that matches the exact description of your car threw a smoke bomb at us and then tried to run us over in the high school parking lot this morning."

"It wasn't me," Stevens said.

"So where were you?"

"At home eating breakfast. Listening to my favorite classical radio station. Does that meet with your approval?"

"I don't suppose anyone can verify that," asked Joe.

"I had breakfast alone, if that's what you're asking. If you want proof—well, I happen to remember this morning's program was Mozart's Requiem."

"That doesn't prove you were at home," Frank said. "You could have been listening on your car radio." He turned to Joe. "It's not much of an alibi, but since we didn't actually see him or the plate number, we can't really pin it on him."

"Come on," Joe said, with a look of disgust. "Let's get out of here."

"Next time you plan on dropping by," Stevens said, "telephone first. I'll be sure to be out."

As the brothers returned to their van, Frank said, "What do you say we head over to Ms. Ziebarth's apartment and see if she's home? It still bothers me that she didn't tell us about that argument with Klingner. And we really don't have any proof of her side of the story."

"That's fine with me," Joe said. "As long as it helps convince you."

They drove over to Ziebarth's apartment building. She didn't answer her buzzer, so Joe had to pick the front-door lock again while Frank acted as lookout. They went upstairs. The apartment door was locked this time so Joe got some more practice with his "dental tools."

Once the lock was picked, Frank swung the door open. The place was a shambles. The futon chair lay on its side, the lamp lay on the floor with its shade crushed, and the desk drawers had been pulled out with their contents scattered across the floor. Even the potted plants lay on their sides, soil spilling onto the rug.

"Somebody was hunting for something," Frank said. "The question is, did they find it? We might as well look through this stuff and see what turns up."

While Frank started sifting through the papers that were strewn around, Joe went into the bedroom, which had also been turned upside down. Closet doors were open. Clothes lay tangled on the floor. Sheets and pillows had been torn off the bed.

Frank, meanwhile, sat down at the desk and turned on the computer.

"Joe," he called into the other room, "I'm going to try getting into her files." He started with the most obvious passwords—her street address and apartment number, then switched-around versions of the same numbers. No luck. On a library card on the floor he saw her birth date and middle name. He tried those, but still no luck. Finally sitting back in the chair to think, he noticed a small scrap of paper amid the jumble on her bulletin board with the word *Nobel* written on it. On a hunch he punched the letters in, and immediately the words *password accepted* flashed onto the screen. Frank shook his head. That was the trouble with these brilliant scientific brains. Sometimes they had no common sense.

Inside the program now, Frank saw research related files as well as lots of E-mail. Ziebarth spent considerable time on-line with people at

Bayport and other universities. Almost all the messages related to her work. There were questions to professors as well as requests to libraries about books and articles. Each message had a transmission time listed among all its formatting codes and address. Frank could see that in the past week Ziebarth had "talked" by computer every morning and almost every night.

Frank heard a rustling behind him. He figured he'd lost track of time while searching Ziebarth's files. It happened all the time when he got on the computer at home.

"So," he said over his shoulder, 'did you find anything?"

As he turned, he glimpsed a figure standing immediately behind him. The person was holding a large rectangular object overhead with two hands. No sooner did he realize that it wasn't Joe than the person brought both arms down hard, smashing him on the head.

# Chapter

## 7

THE BLOW LANDED SOLIDLY, and Frank flopped sideways off Ms. Ziebarth's desk chair. With a loud grunt, he landed in a heap on the carpet.

Joe was still searching her bedroom when he heard the dull thud from the other room. The thud was followed by a louder thud, as if something much bigger had hit the floor. Joe thought maybe Frank had knocked a textbook off its shelf and then set off a chain reaction of books falling down.

"Frank?" Joe called. "Are you okay?"

*"Urghhh,"* came a groan from the other room.

Joe bolted out to the living room.

Frank was on his hands and knees, shaking his head groggily. Beside him lay a fat textbook, splayed open.

"What happened?" Joe asked, bending down to his brother. Frank waved him off, raising one hand and gesturing toward the apartment door, which was ajar.

"Somebody . . ." Frank gasped out. "Go after him . . ."

Joe didn't need to be told twice. He burst into the hallway. It was empty. Sprinting to the elevators, he checked the floor indicators. One of them blinked from a *3* to a *2*. Frank's assailant was on his way down. The other elevator was several floors up. Joe punched the Down button, but the second car continued up. So he went over and yanked the stairwell door open.

Joe flew down the stairs. He fell into a rhythm—step-step-step-*jump*—making the turns on each landing by gripping the railing and whipping himself around each corner. His sneakers squeaked loudly as the floor numbers blurred past: 5 . . . 4 . . . 3 . . . 2 . . . At last he hurled himself at the ground-floor door, yanking on the silver knob and bursting into the lobby. It was also empty.

Joe tore through the lobby and flung open the glass front door. A medium-size green car idled at the curb. A woman driver and two young passengers glanced at him curiously. He bolted down the block and around the corner. By the time he reached the parking garage, there was no one in sight.

Joe turned and walked back toward the

front entrance of the building. He saw Frank coming down the block slowly, stretching his neck and rubbing the back of his head.

"So what do you make of that?" Joe asked after Frank assured him he was okay.

"Whoever it was probably heard you picking the lock and hid in the closet," Frank said.

"Do you think he found what he was after?" Joe said.

"He?" Frank said.

"Well, it wasn't Ms. Ziebarth," Joe said. "She wouldn't have trashed her own apartment and then hit you on the head."

"Probably not," Frank said. "But it's possible. Whoever searched the place is not necessarily the same person who hit me. She could have been hiding in the closet while somebody else searched the place."

"True," Joe admitted. "But I've got to believe it was simpler than that. We surprised somebody who was searching for something in the apartment. The person hit you on the head with one of Ms. Ziebarth's textbooks and got away."

Frank and Joe continued to review possible scenarios on the way home and came to one definite conclusion. Their next step was to figure out what Yvonne Ziebarth had that the assailant wanted.

The next day after the final bell the Hardys stood near the front door of Bayport High

School waiting for Callie and Vanessa, who quickly appeared, bright eyed and smiling.

"Guess what, you guys? We found chemical traces on the label backing," Callie said.

"The PIXE picked up a minute amount," Vanessa said.

"That's great," Frank said. "What is it?"

"Well, that part we haven't figured out yet," Callie admitted.

"But we're close," Vanessa said. She turned to Callie. "After we run that last batch of cross-samples I bet we'll have it."

"Speaking of which," Callie said, "I'd like to stick around and check the readouts."

Joe turned to Frank. "Why don't we head back to Klingner's lab for another look around? You can never go over a crime scene too many times."

"Sounds good," Joe said.

"Why don't I come, too?" Vanessa said. "I could lend a fresh pair of eyes." She turned to Callie. "Is that okay with you, Callie?"

"No problem. I can run the computer-sort myself."

"See you later, then, Callie," Frank said, giving her a quick kiss. "And good luck."

"Wow, this is really impressive," Vanessa said as she took in the university lab. The crime scene tape had been removed and they had no problem talking their way past Mrs.

Barnes. "It's light-years ahead of our school lab. Some of this stuff I don't even recognize. What do you guys expect to find that hasn't been found already?"

"Hard to say," Frank said.

Joe stood at the door to Ziebarth's old office. "We could check around in here."

The trio went into the small room, with its desk, gray metal filing cabinets, desktop computer with monitor and printer, and a neglected-looking plant at the window.

Joe glanced at the empty chair at the computer. "A murderer sat at that keyboard just a few days ago. If only there were some way to glimpse back into the past to see who it was."

Frank stepped forward. "Wait a second," he said. "Maybe there is a way. . . ." Reaching forward, he flipped the computer's red toggle switch. The screen lit up a bluish gray.

"What do you think?" Joe asked. "You're the computer nerds—I mean whizzes. Can you get this electronic crystal ball to tell us who sat here typing that day?"

Frank pulled out the chair and sat down. "Even if it can't tell us who did sit here," he said, "it may tell us the next best thing—who didn't."

Joe blinked. "Huh? Could you spell that out for us?"

For a few seconds Frank's fingers tapped at the keyboard faster than Joe's eyes could follow. Then he stopped to gaze at the screen. "Vanessa, do you see what I see?"

Vanessa studied the display. "I sure do."

"What is it?" Joe said.

Frank raised a hand from the keyboard to tap a finger against the screen. "This software program has a built-in default timed automatic backup option. After a certain amount of time—thirty seconds, a minute, five minutes, whatever it's set for—the program automatically saves the file you're working on. That way you don't lose your data if the machine goes down from an electrical surge, power blackout, or virus attack."

"Or if you just turn off the machine before saving," Vanessa added. "This way your data's still on the hard drive."

"I just called up a list of hard drive files," Frank continued. "As you can see they're listed by name but also by date. See here?" He pointed. "These files were created on the day of Klingner's death. Is there anything that stands out?"

"What about that one?" Joe said. "Untitled. Number One."

"Exactly," Frank said. "Notice it contains only six bytes. Unless I'm way off, I bet I know what six letters those will be."

"But don't you need a password?" Joe asked.

"Not to access these files," Frank said. "Remember, the machine saves them automatically. If you don't name them, they just go under Untitled starting with number one." He looked over his shoulder at Joe and his girlfriend. "Okay, here we go," he said. He tapped several keys to reveal the contents of the file. Within moments the screen glowed with a single word: *oxygen.*

"There it is," Vanessa said. "A word typed by a killer."

"That's it, Joe," Frank said, "exactly what you were looking for—the perfect alibi for Ms. Ziebarth."

# Chapter

# 8

WHAT?" JOE SAID. He and Vanessa turned to look at Frank.

"Remember at Ms. Ziebarth's apartment just before I got clobbered?" Frank said. "When I was sitting at her computer checking her E-mail index? Well, the days and times she was logged on were all recorded. One of those time slots was eight-ten to eight-forty A.M. the morning of Klingner's death. This file was saved at eighty twenty-two A.M. That means, unless Ms. Ziebarth has figured out a way to be in two places at once, she couldn't possibly have been creating a file with the word *oxygen* in it here, while she was logged onto E-mail at home."

"Good work, Frank," Joe said. "But you know what else it means."

"There's a murderer still on the loose," Frank said.

"We've got to take this to Chief Collig and Detective Broussard right away," Joe said. "Let's go."

They drove straight to Bayport Police Headquarters. In the lobby they intercepted Detective Broussard on his way out.

"Let me see if I've got this straight," Broussard said. "You say Ziebarth couldn't have put the label on because she was at home playing on her computer?"

"Not playing," Frank said. "She was on-line, logged onto a network, sending and receiving E-mail. And she has records showing the exact time she sent and received each message."

Broussard scowled. "Ziebarth had motive. She had opportunity, and in my book it'll take more than some numbers on a computer screen to clear her."

"But what we're saying is she didn't have opportunity," Frank said. "When the label was being created in her office at the university, she was at home."

"Yeah, well what if she used her computer to change the records later? I'm sure you guys saw that movie about the kid who uses a home computer to sneak into the Pentagon system and almost start a war.

"Compared to that, this is simple. A scientist

like Ziebarth could doctor the records in about twenty seconds."

Frank shook his head. "First, Ms. Ziebarth would have to be a hacker supreme to manage that—"

" 'Hacker supreme'?" Broussard said.

"A computer genius," Frank said, "which Ms. Ziebarth isn't. She's a research chemist."

Broussard waved his hand dismissively. "A scientist is a scientist in my book," he said.

Frank flashed Joe an exasperated look. Broussard was a complete dinosaur when it came to technology.

"And second," Frank continued, "she couldn't have changed the times because the network keeps its own records. Even if she changed them on her home machine, the phone company records would be almost impossible to change. We're sure if you double-check that way it will confirm she was home."

"I'm still not buying it," Broussard said to Frank. "For all I know, she wrote those messages ahead of time then had the computer send them automatically while she was typing the label in the lab."

"Impossible," Frank said. "Ziebarth was in conferring mode, which means she and her colleagues were typing back and forth, live."

"Maybe someone else used her computer," Broussard said. "She could have had an accomplice. As far as I'm concerned, she's still our number one suspect.

Broussard said, "Sorry, fellas, but I've got to go—dinnertime."

"Come on, Frank and Vanessa," Joe said. "I could stand some dinner, too. Let's call Callie and see if she wants to meet us at Mr. Pizza. My treat."

"So, you ready to order?"

Tony Prito stood beside their red- and white-checked covered table, his hands white with flour, his apron smelling of pizza dough. Mr. Pizza was the Hardys' favorite pizza parlor because it served a generous-size slice for a good price but also because their friend Tony worked there.

"We'll have a large with the works, Tony," said Frank. "Leave out the anchovies on half of it."

"Expecting Callie?" Tony said, winking as he went back behind the counter. He knew from experience how Callie felt about anchovies.

A couple of minutes later Callie and Yvonne Ziebarth arrived.

"Sure smells good in here," Ms. Ziebarth said as the Hardys and the two girls made room for her at their booth. When everyone was seated, Frank started right in.

"So, let's go over who the suspects are," he asked. "First, we have to consider opportunity—who had the chance to print that label and stick it on the phosgene canister?"

"Stevens, of course," said Joe.

"Lots of other people, too," Vanessa said.

"Starting with Koo," Frank said. "His office is just up the hall from Klingner's lab."

"Actually," Vanessa said, "just about anyone in the chemistry department could have figured out a way into Ms. Ziebarth's office and the lab."

"So maybe looking for opportunity isn't the best way to approach this," Joe said.

"Okay," Frank said, "what about motive? Who had a reason to want Klingner dead?"

"Stevens again," Joe said.

"Come on, Joe," Ms. Ziebarth said. "Marcus is just a kid. That's impossible."

"Not necessarily. He obviously . . ." For once Joe tried to pick his words carefully. "Well, I think he might have a—he might have a crush on you, Ms. Ziebarth. Maybe he thought he was avenging you by sabotaging the man who stole your work."

"There's no way Marcus would kill anybody, Joe," she said. "And what's this about his having a crush on me?"

Joe shrugged. "I don't know, it's just a guess."

They speculated some more on Stevens's possible motives. Ziebarth refused to believe her friend was capable of murder or any other crime for that matter. Even Joe had to admit that the evidence against Stevens was circumstantial. If only he and Frank hadn't missed identifying whoever was driving the red car in the parking lot.

"What about professional reasons?" Callie said. "Someone wanting to steal Klingner's research or ruin his reputation, say."

"That makes sense," Frank said. "If someone's after Klingner's research secrets, they might also go after Ms. Ziebarth, which would explain why they trashed her apartment."

"But not why they killed Klingner," Callie said. "They wouldn't have to kill him to steal his research."

"If he found out what was going on," Vanessa said, "and if those secrets were valuable enough, they might have."

Right after dinner Joe noticed that Ms. Ziebarth was studying her watch. "I should be getting home," she said. "What with all the time I've been spending at the police station and my lawyer's office, I've been ignoring my work. I've got to get back to analyzing that data. The more we speculate, the more I realize it may be the key to this whole case. If I can figure out exactly what Dr. Klingner saw in that data, then maybe it'll tell us why he was killed."

"And who killed him, too," Joe said. "Or at least it could help us narrow down the list of suspects."

Callie said she'd drive Vanessa home so the

boys could drive Ms. Ziebarth back to her apartment. At first she politely refused, saying she'd call a cab, but with a little friendly insistence they were able to convince her.

"First of all," Frank said, "it's dangerous. Klingner's murderer is still out there somewhere."

"And besides," Joe said, "your apartment's probably still a mess. We could help you clean up a little while you get to work on that data."

It took them less than fifteen minutes to reach Ms. Ziebarth's apartment building. It was quiet on her block at that time of the evening. They took the elevator up. On the way, Frank said, "We need to take it slowly when we get upstairs. A little extra caution never hurt anybody."

Moments later they had made their way quietly down the hallway to Ms. Ziebarth's apartment door. Frank and Joe stood on each side of her, their silhouettes framing the door as she fit her key into the lock. They were both turned sideways, knees slightly bent. They wanted to be ready to meet whoever or whatever was waiting for them inside the apartment.

Ms. Ziebarth glanced quickly at Joe and then at Frank. They both nodded, and she turned the key before pushing open the door. Instantly, they were greeted by a tremendous rush of scorching hot air and a deafening boom that lifted all three of them off their feet.

# Chapter

## 9

THE FORCE OF THE BLAST was enough to throw both Frank and Joe hard against the opposite wall, knocking the breath out of them.

Joe found himself on his back with something large, heavy, and flat lying across his chest. His ears were ringing, and his eyes stung. The next moment he realized that something under him was stirring. It was his brother.

"Joe," Frank said. "Are you all right?"

A lot of smoke was swirling out of the apartment and around the hallway. "I think so," Joe answered, and immediately started coughing.

"Well, get off me. I think Ms. Ziebarth's under me."

Joe snapped to. He pushed at the heavy object on top of him and saw that it was the apartment door, blown clean off its hinges. He shoved it aside and struggled to his feet.

"Ms. Ziebarth," Joe exclaimed, "are you okay?" Back on their feet, the brothers helped Joe's teacher up. She was coughing and couldn't speak at first. "What happened?"

"Hard to say," Frank said. "It could have been a bomb. First things first, though. How do you feel?"

"I'm all right. I think I just—ouch!" She was trying to straighten up when she grimaced and shot a hand to the small of her back.

"Ms. Ziebarth," Frank said, "I think we'd better get you to the emergency room."

"I don't think that'll be—" She shook her head, then winced and grabbed the back of her neck.

"Frank's right," said Joe. "You need to get some X rays."

A hazy rectangle of light showed through the dust and smoke down the hallway. One of the neighbors opened his door and poked his head out. "What's happening?" he asked. "Who's out there?"

"Sir, there's been an explosion," Frank replied. "Would you please call Nine-one-one?"

"Right away," the man answered.

Minutes later the Hardys stood with a group of tenants on the sidewalk outside the building. There were police and fire trucks and an ambulance, all with lights flashing, parked out front.

Two paramedics wheeled Yvonne Ziebarth past on a gurney. She looked pale but was able to manage a weak smile for Frank and Joe. "I guess Joe was right about the place being a mess," she said. "Will I see you at the hospital?"

Frank and Joe promised they'd stop by after they'd finished with the police. No sooner did the ambulance drive away than an unmarked police car pulled up. It had a red light flashing on the dashboard. Detective Broussard climbed out of the car. He spotted the Hardys right away and walked toward them.

"Uh-oh," Joe said, under his breath. "There goes our night."

"Any time there's trouble, I can count on you two to show up," Broussard said, annoyance crossing his face.

A fire marshal passed by, and ignoring the detective, Frank turned to speak to him. "Excuse me, sir," he said. "Any idea what caused the explosion?"

The man stopped to buckle his coat. He took a look at the Hardys and at Detective Broussard. "Probably gas," he said. "We see them like this all the time. People forget to turn their stoves off all the way or there's a leak somewhere."

"What could have triggered it?" asked Joe.

"If the apartment was filled with gas, it could have been the refrigerator kicking on or some other switch—anything that makes even a tiny spark."

"Any idea when you'll have final results of your investigation?" Frank asked.

"All right, that's enough," Broussard interrupted. "We're going to let this gentleman go about his business," the detective said with a jerk of his thumb toward the fire marshal, "and you boys are going to tell me exactly what happened up there.

"I want a blow-by-blow of where you were, what you did, and who you talked to from the time you left police headquarters to the time of the explosion." The detective pulled out his small notepad from his jacket pocket, took out a pen, and got ready to start taking notes.

"We had dinner at Mr. Pizza with some friends," Joe said.

"What friends?" Broussard said.

"Well, there was Callie Shaw, Vanessa Bender, and Ms. Ziebarth," Frank said.

"A regular chemistry convention," Broussard said, with a smile. "And I suppose the topic of conversation was molecular bonding or maybe the nature of solutions?"

"No, actually we were trying to come up with a list of suspects other than Ms. Ziebarth," Frank said.

"Considering she was with you that was very

polite," Broussard said. "So who else did you add to your list?"

"Anybody who could have had access to the chem department and who might have had a reason to be jealous of Professor Klingner—personally or professionally."

"Did Ziebarth have anything to say about any other suspects?" Broussard asked.

"Not really," Frank said. "She was anxious to get back to her data. She seemed to think it might be the key to a murder motive."

"Did Ziebarth say anything else other than wanting to get back to analyzing her data?" the detective continued.

"No, sir," Frank said.

"All right, I can see this is going nowhere," Broussard said, tapping his pen on his notepad. "Let's talk about what happened after you left the pizza parlor...."

Broussard questioned the brothers for another fifteen minutes. He made them retrace their every step after they left Mr. Pizza. Once he was satisfied he had a complete statement about the explosion, he sent them on their way with another warning to stay out of police business.

The first thing the Hardys did when they got to the van was call the hospital on their cellular phone. There were no visiting hours until nine A.M. the next day. Ms. Ziebarth would be admitted to the hospital, the receptionist told them, but she didn't have a room number yet so they'd have to check back later. Frank and Joe were both feeling a little banged up from the explosion themselves so they decided to go home, rest, and get back on the case first thing in the morning.

The next day was Saturday so Frank and Joe headed straight to the hospital after breakfast.

"I hope Ms. Ziebarth feels better than I do," Joe said, rubbing the back of his neck as they walked toward the main entrance of Bayport General Hospital. "Getting that door in the face wasn't much fun. Remind me never to take a job as a door-to-door salesman."

"Actually, that door probably saved you from the worst of the blast," Frank said.

"So what do you think, Frank?" Joe said. "Was it just bad luck? Nothing but a little old gas leak, or maybe Ms. Ziebarth forgot to turn off her stove?"

"If you're thinking what I'm thinking, Joe," Frank said, "we had better check out that apartment again before we chalk it up to just another accident."

When they got to the hospital, the receptionist gave them directions to Yvonne Ziebarth's room, Number 310. They rode the elevator with nurses holding clipboards and doctors in baggy green scrubs, their stethoscopes dangling around their necks.

"This way," Joe said, following the arrows as they got out on the third floor. Joe went down the hallway and was about to knock on the door of 310 when a nurse came out pushing an old woman in a wheelchair. The brothers stepped aside to let them pass. Then they heard a familiar voice. It was coming from behind the curtain room divider inside. "I appreciate your coming to visit, but I'll be out in a day or so. You shouldn't have bothered." It was Yvonne Ziebarth's voice.

"Actually, I had another reason for coming by," replied a man's voice. It was Professor Holt. "I thought you might consider coming to work for me. I could use someone with your abilities. Your friend Marcus Stevens works for me now, so things no doubt would run smoothly."

"Well, that's kind of you, Dr. Holt, but is there enough work for three assistants?"

"Three? Actually, it would be just two: you and Marcus."

"What about Tang Ly Koo? I thought he was with you, too."

"He *was*," Holt said, pausing for effect. "Until the other day."

"Did he leave?"

"Disappeared is more like it. I've never heard of anyone vanishing so suddenly. I arrived at the lab yesterday, and all his things were gone: his personal possessions, research data, everything. When he didn't show up for work, I called his home number. There was a phone company recording saying the line had been disconnected with no forwarding number."

"Have you notified the police?" Ziebarth asked.

"Yes, of course. This coming so soon after Klingner's death, it was the first thing I did. They said they'd look into it. To be honest, I think it sounds very suspicious, but I'll leave that to the police. I hope it all turns out fine, but in the meantime I need a replacement—someone with experience."

"I'm definitely interested," Ms. Ziebarth said. "Would you mind if I think about it for a day or so?"

"Not at all. I presume you'll want to finish up teaching at the high school. I was thinking of your starting at the summer term." There was a pause. "I should get back to work and let you have some rest."

The Hardys heard the sound of a chair scraping on the tile floor and loose change jingling in a pocket. Professor Holt was getting up to leave.

Frank cleared his throat loudly and called over his shoulder, "Here it is, Joe. Room Three-Ten."

Picking up the cue, Joe said, "Right, here we are." They stepped into the room, and Joe said, "Ms. Ziebarth?" as they peeked around the curtain. "Oh, hello, Professor Holt."

"Hello," Holt said, offering Joe his hand. "Nice to see you again. I was just on my way out."

"Now, you'll think about my offer, won't you?" the professor said to Ms. Ziebarth. With that he gave a little wave of his hand, turned, and left.

"How are you feeling, Ms. Ziebarth?" Joe asked.

"Better," she said. "The X rays were all negative. I'm just bruised. They'll probably let me go later today."

"Nice of Dr. Holt to visit," Joe said.

"Yes. He offered me a job. He said I could start in June. School's out, so I'll need a job then anyway."

They spent the next ten minutes chatting about Ms. Ziebarth's hospital stay. Although she was grateful for the chance to rest, she was also anxious to go home.

"Just lying around here," she said, "I get nervous about all the work I'm missing. I feel like I should be out there accomplishing something."

"We were going to stop by your apartment," Joe said. "The cops think the explosion was an accident, but we'd like to check it out a little more carefully. Is there anything we can pick up for you there?"

"Definitely," Ziebarth said. "See if you can find the hard drive from my computer. Most of my research data is on there. I hope it's not too damaged to recover."

"No problem," said Frank.

In the van on the way to Ms. Ziebarth's apartment, Joe said, "Koo's disappearing sure is suspicious. I'd say it moves him right to the top of the suspect list."

"I don't know if I'd go that far," Frank said.

"Think about it," Joe said. "Klingner's murdered, then Koo disappears without a trace. Koo worked in a lab right next to Klingner. What if he stole research secrets from Klingner."

"That's all guesswork, Joe," Frank said. "We don't have any evidence. Do you think Koo would be capable of killing Klingner?"

"As Vanessa said, maybe he had to do it to keep him quiet," Joe said. "Koo could be an industrial spy. Klingner's research secrets could be worth tens of millions of dollars. He could be halfway to China carrying that information in his briefcase by now!"

Frank held an imaginary microphone up to his mouth and said, "Earth to Joe, Earth to Joe—Joe, do you read me?"

"What, Frank?" Joe snapped.

"Sorry, but I think your theory sounds a little far-fetched," Frank said.

"I'm willing to bet you money that's exactly

what we find out when the smoke clears," Joe said.

Frank didn't answer. He just kept driving for a few minutes, seemingly lost in his thoughts. "Speaking of smoke," he finally said, "I just realized something. When Detective Broussard was questioning us, we told him the explosion happened when we got to the apartment. We didn't tell him it happened right when we opened the door. Even if Ms. Ziebarth forgot to turn off the gas, what are the chances it would blow up precisely when we opened the door?"

"Good point, Frank," Joe said. "Now, as you would say, all we need is some solid evidence."

When the elevator door slid open on Yvonne Ziebarth's floor, the boys saw the lights were on, and although there was still a slight smoky smell, the air was clear. There was a piece of plywood, secured with a heavy latch and padlock, where Ms. Ziebarth's door had been.

Frank tilted his head toward the lock. "Joe, why don't you pretend that's my locker at school and I've got the answers to your next algebra exam inside?" he said.

Joe grinned at his brother's challenge. Pulling out his "dental probes," he got to work. Frank checked his watch as Joe worked on the lock. Soon a sharp click sounded and the lock shackle jumped free.

"One minute and forty-five seconds," Frank said. "I guess you're a little out of practice."

"Hey, I'd like to see you beat that," Joe said.

"Okay, okay," his brother said, "don't sweat it. We're in and that's what counts."

Frank nudged the board aside, and the brothers peered in. The apartment was pitch-dark except for whatever light was coming from the hallway behind them.

"Wait a minute," Frank said. He took a small flashlight out of his pocket, flicked it on, and played its thin but powerful beam around inside the apartment.

The blast must have blown out the windows because sheets of plywood were fitted there, too. The walls were blackened, which made the place seem even darker. Joe tried the light switch but nothing happened.

"The electric company probably cut the power until the apartment's declared safe again," he said.

Frank surveyed the apartment and said, "This place looks like a bomb went off."

Joe chuckled. It was what their mother said about Joe's room every time he left it a mess. "Very funny," he said. "Are we really going to have to search the whole place with a penlight?"

"We may not have to,". Frank said. "Let's start by re-creating what happened."

"Simple," Joe said. "We opened the door and boom."

"Exactly. So the trigger must have been connected to the front door."

Frank trained the beam on the door frame just above their heads. "Even a tiny battery and switch could make a big enough spark," he said.

They both checked in and around the door frame for electrical switches, wires, or pieces of electrical tape, anything that could point to the source of the spark.

"Look," Joe said, pointing to a dark object in the flashlight beam along the door frame. "What's that?"

Taped along the inside of the door frame where the door latch would have been was a small, gritty, black strip. The brothers examined it closely. Frank was the first to recognize it. "It's the friction tape from a book of matches," he said. "You know, where you strike the match head."

"That's got to be what triggered the explosion," Joe said.

"Someone turns on the gas in the apartment," Frank said. "They attach the strip there and put two or three matches against it wedged between the door and the frame. They leave, and the next person who opens the door—boom!"

"So there's our proof," Joe said. "It wasn't an accident. It was attempted murder."

"There's definitely a killer on the loose," Frank said. "He killed Klingner, he went after us, and now he's trying to kill Ms. Ziebarth."

# Chapter

# 10

JOE GRABBED HIS BROTHER'S SLEEVE. "Come on, Frank," he said. "Let's take that strip and pay a visit to Chief Collig."

"Don't forget about Ms. Ziebarth's hard drive," Frank said.

They went back into the charred apartment and found her computer, which had been knocked off the desk by the blast. The case was partly cracked open. With the help of a small hammer and a Phillips head screwdriver they found in one of the kitchen drawers, Frank and Joe were able to open up the computer and pull out its hard drive. The unit looked battered and charred, but worth trying to salvage.

Twenty minutes later the brothers, carrying

their evidence, pulled their van up to the police station. Within a few minutes, they stood inside Chief Collig's office door.

The Bayport police chief spent a few seconds turning the gritty, narrow black strip in his fingers before flipping it back onto his desk. "Of all the wild, crazy stories," he said, shaking his head. "Boys, do you really expect me to swallow a yarn like that?"

The Hardys stared at the police chief across his big wooden desk. They were still standing because the chief hadn't offered them chairs. Behind them, Detective Broussard leaned against the door frame.

"Chief, our theory makes perfect sense," Joe said. "How and why else could that explosion have been set off?"

"According to you someone's trying to kill Yvonne Ziebarth," Collig said. "They killed Klingner, and now they're after her. Well, answer me this—who is it and why are they doing it?"

"We have a few ideas," Joe said. "But—"

"We don't know," Frank admitted. "We think Ms. Ziebarth's research data may be the key. If she can figure out exactly what Klingner was onto, maybe we can establish a motive for the killing."

The chief picked up a stack of papers from his desk. "Boys"—Joe hated it when he called them that, and he was convinced the chief did it purposely to annoy them—"right here I've got a desk full of cases. And since I'm not convinced Ms. Ziebarth's not guilty I don't see the point of wasting time on more suspects. Until you give me hard evidence of all your theories, they'll remain just that—theories." He shook his head. "The fire department has determined that the gas in her apartment was turned on. The way I see it, she turned it on and forgot about it. Maybe she was distracted. She already admitted she was upset and forgot to lock her door, so she could just as easily have forgotten about the gas. It was an accident, pure and simple."

"But how do you explain the matchbook strike-strip?" asked Frank.

Collig squinted at them. "Now, I'm not accusing you of anything *yet*, but Detective Broussard here told me you two are pretty cozy with Ms. Ziebarth. He says you're working pretty hard to prove she's innocent. If I were ever to catch you offering phony evidence or planting anything at a crime scene . . ."

"Chief Collig," Joe said, "we would never even think of doing anything like that."

"Chief," Frank said, "what would it take to convince you that someone's out to kill the chemists at Bayport University?"

"Forget it, boys," he said. "I've got to get back to work." Collig stood up and began ushering them toward the door. "Take care of yourselves now, and stay out of our way so we can do our job."

"What about that grad student who's missing?" Joe blurted out. "Tang Ly Koo."

"What do you know about that?" the chief snapped. He glared at his detective. "Broussard, that's supposed to be confidential."

"I didn't say anything." The detective shrugged his thick shoulders. He turned toward the brothers. "How do you two know about Koo?"

"I'm sorry," Frank said, "but we've got to protect our source. Unless you have a court order forcing us to give it up."

"Koo is right at the top of our suspect list," Joe said, "and we have reason to believe he was a foreign industrial spy."

"That's ridiculous," Broussard said.

"That's it," Collig said, pointing out the door with both hands. "You two are outta here. We can track down Mr. Koo just fine without any amateur help." Broussard took Frank and Joe each by an elbow and escorted them out into the hall, then he turned and went back into Collig's office without a word.

Outside, on the way to the van, Frank said, "Joe, 'we have reason to believe Koo is a foreign industrial spy'? I thought you got over that one. I didn't think you were going to try it out on them."

"I figured if I sprung that on them they

might leak some more information," Joe said. "The worst they were going to do was kick us out."

"Which they did," Frank said.

"And they pretty much admitted that Koo is on their list," Joe said. "So my theory isn't so far-fetched after all."

"Koo has got to be high up on anybody's suspect list at this point," Frank said.

"Let's not forget about Stevens," Joe said. "If we could tie him to the smoke bomb attack in the parking lot—"

"And the whack on my head in Ms. Ziebarth's apartment, *and* the explosion there," Frank said. "I don't know about him. He definitely has the know-how to build all kinds of bombs, but he would have to be a serious psycho to try to kill Ms. Ziebarth. She's his friend."

"Who knows? If he killed Klingner and now he realizes we're after him," Joe said, "he might feel backed into a corner. It might have driven him crazy enough to do anything."

"Let's head back over to the university," Frank said. "We can stake out the science building again and maybe find Stevens or Koo or both of them."

On the way over, they used their cellular phone to call Ms. Ziebarth at the hospital. They arranged to pick her up that afternoon and suggested that she spend some time at Vanessa's place. Vanessa lived on an old farm with her mother, who had converted the barn into a state-of-the-art computer animation studio for her business. Ms. Ziebarth's apartment was going to need more than a spring cleaning, and with her computer expertise, Vanessa could help Ms. Ziebarth recover the data from her hard drive in the relative safety and quiet of the farm.

One more call and they had confirmed the arrangement with Vanessa and her mom. Vanessa was eager to help in any way she could.

Frank pulled into the science building parking lot at the university and took a spot near the back. He and Joe walked over to the building and were about to step inside when Joe suddenly grabbed his shoulder. Frank stopped in his tracks.

"Look," Joe said.

Following Joe's gaze, Frank spotted a familiar figure with thick glasses waiting at the elevators down the hall. He was carrying an empty cardboard carton.

"Stevens," Frank said in a loud whisper. "What do you think he's up to with that box?"

"Only one way to find out," Joe said. Stevens got on one of the elevators. The Hardys went over to it and watched the dial rotate to three. Joe reached for the button, but Frank stopped him.

"Let's give him a minute or two to start

whatever he came for," Frank said. "Then we take him by surprise."

Padding down the semidark hallway moments later, Joe whispered, "It sure is quiet today."

At the end of the hallway, they saw a light shining through the frosted glass door of Professor Holt's lab. When they got closer they heard the sound of drawers opening and closing, the thump of books being stacked, and the sharp snap of cabinet doors opening and slamming. Someone was either angry or in a hurry.

"He sounds awfully busy in there," whispered Joe.

"Let's find out what he's doing," Frank said.

The brothers shoved open the door, and a surprised Stevens turned to face them. He was standing at a lab table with a carton on top of it. The box was half-filled with notebooks, computer diskettes, loose papers, a small wall calendar, and a coffee mug. In his hand was a small box of diskettes, which he was about to drop into the carton along with everything else.

"What do you want now?" he asked. "What are you doing here?"

"We should be asking you the same question," Joe said. Nodding toward the carton, he continued, "That's a funny kind of research to be doing on a Saturday when no one's around."

Stevens scowled and dropped the diskettes into the carton. "My days of research here are through. Holt fired me. I'm just collecting my belongings."

"Fired you?" Frank asked. "When? Why?"

Stevens shook his head. "Yesterday afternoon," he said. "As for why . . ." He shrugged. The Hardys waited. Stevens finally said, "Well, all right. I was snooping around his desk, and he caught me."

"Snooping for what?"

"Anything that would help me find Koo. He's obviously the key."

"What did Holt say?" Frank asked.

"He asked if I was in cahoots with Koo. Then he said I'd better pack up and leave."

"Are you?" asked Joe.

"Am I what?" Stevens's face flushed an angry red.

"Are you in cahoots with Koo?" Joe said.

"What are you talking about?" Stevens countered. "What kind of accusation is that?"

Frank tried to calm him down. "Now, Marcus, don't get excited. Joe only meant to ask—"

"I heard what he asked. He accused me of being in league with Koo. He thinks we both killed Klingner and framed Yvonne." Stevens pounded his fist against the table. "Well, it so happens I had nothing to do with any of this—nothing! And you listen to me. I will get to the bottom of this. I will find Koo. I will follow him all the way to China if I have to."

With that Marcus snatched up his carton and stormed out the door, leaving the Hardys staring after him.

"Super-Nerd's a regular wild man once he gets riled, isn't he?" Joe said.

"The mild-mannered lab scientist who turns into a monster," Frank said. "It's an old story."

"Dr. Jekyll and Mr. Hyde, I believe," Joe said.

"What do you think, Joe? Is he working with Koo? You saw how angry he got just at the suggestion."

Joe frowned. "I saw how angry he *seemed* to get. What if he was acting to throw us off?"

"Could be . . ." Frank said, but he didn't finish the rest of his thought because he heard a faint hissing sound coming from under the lab table where Stevens had been packing his box.

"Joe, do you hear that?" Frank said. The sound was growing louder. Frank turned toward Stevens's table. Then he wrinkled his nose. "That smell," he said.

"It's like rotten eggs," Joe said, instinctively putting his hand to his nose.

Within a second or two, they knew they were in trouble. A large yellow-gray cloud of smoke billowed out from under the table. Noxious fumes filled the room, and Joe gasped for breath as his throat and nostrils started to burn.

# Chapter

# 11

"FRANK, HOLD YOUR BREATH," Joe shouted, already half-blinded by the cloud of thick smoke filling the room. His eyes felt as if hot sand were in them. He staggered forward, barely able to see a foot in front of him.

"Frank," he rasped, coughing. He took another step and immediately knocked into something that crashed to the floor. Glass fragments exploded against his pant legs, and when he took his next step, shards crunched beneath his sneakers.

Joe could hear his brother coughing hard. "Frank, hold your breath," he croaked again. But by the sound of it, Frank had already coughed all the air out of his lungs.

Whatever type of gas it was, Joe knew it was

powerful. It had only taken a small, bitter whiff to seize his chest like a vise. It wasn't the sweet smell of phosgene, but it could be something just as deadly. He knew he might only have a few more seconds to act. His eyes tightly closed and tearing, he spun and immediately bumped into a chair, feeling it bite his shin. He grabbed the back of the chair tightly with both hands and forced his eyes open. The burning in his eyes felt like liquid soap, only a hundred times worse. Sensing the pale light from the windows, he jerked the chair high overhead, stepped forward, and hurled it with all his strength.

The chair flew out of Joe's hands into the swirling cloud of smoke. There was an instant of silence followed by the loud crash of glass shattering. Joe felt a rush of air around him even as he slipped on some spilled liquid and came down hard on his hands and knees. He heard glass fragments tinkling on the cement outside and then the crunch of splintering wood as the chair hit the pavement.

The whole room seemed to move toward the light. Joe realized it wasn't the room, of course, but the smoke being sucked out the open window. Joe could feel the poisonous smoke rushing past as he pulled himself to his feet.

"Frank," he said, his voice grating. Immediately he fell into a coughing fit. But then he felt a strong grip on his arm.

"Come on," Frank said close to Joe's ear. "We've got to get out." Now that they could make out shapes, they stumbled and slipped toward the door, which Frank flung open. The hallway outside seemed incredibly clear. They blinked, wiped their eyes, and grasped their knees as they gulped fresh air.

The poisonous smoke was following them out into the hallway, so Frank slammed the door. Only a tiny amount seeped out now. They made their way down the hallway still short of breath. Joe grabbed the handle of the red fire alarm box on the wall and jerked it down.

The fire alarm went off. It was a deafening electronic buzz that echoed up and down the hall like a million angry hornets. The brothers jogged toward the stairs where a door flew open. A young woman in a white lab coat stood there staring and mouthing the words, "What's going on?" Joe seized her arm and pulled her into the stairwell after them.

Outside, perhaps a dozen people stood milling around in lab coats over jeans and T-shirts, gawking up at the building. Because it was Saturday, the building was almost empty.

They could all hear the wail of sirens approaching. Everyone stared up at the gaping hole where the third-floor window had been. There were traces of yellowish smoke billowing out from it into the sky.

Joe and Frank leaned against a car and breathed deeply.

"Get ready for another inquisition," Frank panted, nodding toward the emergency vehicles pulling up.

The first vehicles—a campus security car, two fire engines, and a Bayport city police car—screeched to a stop. The firefighters, wearing oxygen tanks over their heavy coats, hurried straight into the building, while one uniformed police office and one campus officer asked if anyone knew what had happened.

Frank raised his hand. "Over here," he said.

He and Joe were describing what had happened when a white station wagon rolled up. Professor Holt climbed out and walked over to the police, who were questioning the Hardys.

"Does anybody know what happened?" Holt asked. "I got a call at home from the campus police."

A fire captain came over to the group and said, "Dr. Holt, would you please come up with us to the lab? We're checking for damage and trying to determine the cause of this."

"Of course," Holt said. "Let's go." The Hardys and one of the campus police officers went along.

Once they were upstairs, Holt said, "Well, the cause is obvious. That smell of rotten eggs is sulfuric acid. If you mix it with water, it superheats beyond its boiling point and releases a deadly gas."

"We were inside here when it happened," Joe said as they approached the lab. "Smoke just started billowing out from under that counter."

"What were you doing here?" Holt said.

"We were with Marcus Stevens when he came in to clear out his things," Frank said.

"You two had no right to be in this laboratory," Holt said. "I doubt you have the proper training to deal with chemicals. And anyway, you're not even students at the university."

"Not students?" the campus police officer said. "I want a word with you two. We may have to charge you with trespassing."

Dr. Holt eyed the brothers. "You were in this lab where you weren't supposed to be and you claim this cloud of smoke just happened?" he said. "Chemicals don't just go mixing themselves, gentlemen. Are you sure you weren't handling materials in here?"

"No way," said Joe.

"We never touched anything," Frank said.

"All right, boys," the campus cop said. "If you want to get out of this you're going to have to come up with a little more detail than that." With help from the fire captain and Professor Holt, the cop went on to question Frank and Joe about their confrontation with Marcus, about Marcus's sudden exit from the lab, and about the poison gas cloud that followed. The Hardys gave a blow-by-blow account and finally, after a half hour of questioning, they convinced the police to let them go.

Climbing back into their van in the parking lot, Joe said, "How much do you want to bet Stevens set that up?"

"It looks that way, doesn't it?" Frank said. "Let's go over to his apartment and see if we can finally get some straight answers out of him."

They drove over to Stevens's place in Greenfield, parked on the street, and were mildly surprised when Stevens buzzed them up.

When Stevens swung open his apartment door, he acted almost resigned to the Hardys' being there. "I'm getting awfully tired of you guys following me around," he said. Joe noticed he was wearing his thick black suspenders instead of a belt again.

The brothers followed Stevens into his apartment, sat down on the sofa, and described what had just happened at the lab. Stevens's surprise appeared to be genuine, but Frank knew that that meant nothing: criminals were often excellent actors.

"That smoke attack at the lab wasn't something you rigged up, was it, Marcus?" Joe asked.

"Come on. Do you think I'd be sitting here

talking to you right now if it was?" Stevens said.

"How do you account for it, then?" Joe said. "There wasn't anyone else around at the time."

"How could I have known you'd be in the lab?" Marcus said. He was starting to heat up again—it didn't take much. "I'm trying to pursue my own investigation into this, if that's all right with you. I'm trying to clear my name."

"It's just another really big coincidence," Frank said. "First the red car with the smoke bomb and now this. We're just trying to put some pieces together."

"Well, you don't seem to be making any progress, do you?" said Stevens, standing up, his voice cracking. "I've told you enough times already. I don't know anything about these attacks. So why do you keep harassing me?" Stevens turned and as he went into the kitchen said, "I want this to stop!"

Frank gave Joe a look. "Do you think he's got something on the stove?"

The next moment Stevens came rushing back into the living room holding a kitchen fire extinguisher out with both arms. Stevens aimed the nozzle at the Hardys, his finger on the lever. "Now get out of here and leave me alone!"

"Calm down, Stevens," Joe said. "Are you crazy?"

"I said get out!" Stevens shouted.

"Come on, Joe," Frank said, turning toward the door. "We've wasted enough time on him for one day."

"Do you believe that guy?" Frank said, shaking his head as the brothers climbed into the van.

"I don't call him Super-Nerd for nothing," Joe said. "Let's just hope he outgrows it sometime in the next twenty or thirty years."

"It's just as well we left," Frank said, glancing at his watch. "We've got to go pick up Ms. Ziebarth."

Joe's teacher was sitting in a wheelchair with a nurse beside her, waiting for them at the main entrance to the hospital. She was obviously eager to leave.

"Hi, guys," she said as they drove up. "Right on time." She waved goodbye to the nurse, climbed into the van, and said, "I really want to thank you for setting this up with Vanessa and her mother."

"No problem," said Joe.

"We also brought you this," Frank said, reaching into the backseat and handing her a small cardboard box that contained the hard disk from her computer.

"Great," she said. "I've been thinking about getting back to my research. I feel good about it. I think I may be on the verge of a breakthrough."

They sat back to enjoy the half-hour drive to the Benders'. It was a warm, clear day and they had the windows rolled down. Joe turned on the radio. Soon they were outside the city, cruising down a quiet country road.

There was almost no traffic. Once, Frank caught a glimpse of a car in his rearview mirror about a half-mile back.

A few minutes later, along a deserted stretch of roadway, Frank saw another car in his rearview mirror. It was a small red sedan, and it was approaching fast.

As the sound of its engine grew louder, Frank saw the car swerve into the passing lane and race up beside them on their left. He heard the car's engine revving loudly, but he also heard several sharp reports that were even louder.

"I think we're backfiring," Ms. Ziebarth said, with a slight note of concern in her voice.

"That's not backfire," Joe said. "Those are gunshots."

## Chapter

# 12

"GET DOWN!" Frank shouted.

Joe, who was in the backseat, leaned forward to shove Ms. Ziebarth out of the line of fire.

Frank, meanwhile, hit the brakes. The van lurched and skidded, tires screeching as the red car sped past.

"Hold on," Frank said. As soon as he controlled the skid, he floored the gas pedal.

"What's happening?" Ms. Ziebarth said.

"Stay down," Joe said.

The van tore after the other vehicle, following for half a mile or so until Frank seemed satisfied. "Okay, all clear," he said, slowly, pulling onto the shoulder. The car kept going and disappeared around a bend.

"Is everyone all right?" Frank asked.

"I'm fine," Joe said. "Ms. Ziebarth?"

"I'm okay," she said, straightening up and brushing her hair out of her eyes. "Don't you guys ever have a quiet moment? No sooner do I leave the hospital after nearly getting blown up than I'm ducking bullets."

"We're just a thrill a minute," Joe said. "Frank, it was that red car. Did you see the driver?"

"No," Frank replied. "But I did get the plate number. It was 7BE-453."

Joe grabbed a pad and pen from the glove compartment. "Number 7BE-453," he said as he wrote. "I didn't think you'd miss it again, Frank."

As they got out of the van to check for damage, Ms. Ziebarth asked, "What did you two mean about it being that red car?"

Joe turned to her. "It was the same make, model, year, and color as Marcus Stevens's car. We never saw the plate number when he almost ran us down in the high school parking lot. Now we've got it."

Ziebarth frowned. "Joe, do you still think Marcus is behind any of this?"

"We won't have to guess anymore," Frank said. "Once we know who this plate's registered to, we'll know who shot at us."

Joe was examining the driver's-side door. "Check these out," he said. Three dime-size holes had been punched into the metal door, two above the handle and a third below.

"We're lucky they didn't go all the way through," Ziebarth said.

"A high-caliber slug like a forty-five automatic or forty-four magnum might," said Frank. "There's a lot of metal inside these doors—structural beams, reinforcement panels, gears for raising and lowering the windows— so it's pretty iffy whether a small one could get clear through or not."

They climbed back into the van, started up, and headed for the Benders' farm again. As they pulled around the bend at the end of the straightaway, there was a metallic rattling sound.

"What was that?" Ms. Ziebarth said.

"Good news," Frank said. "The bullets are still inside the door. As long as they're not too flattened out from the impact, the police lab should be able to trace them."

"If they have a gun to match them to," Joe added.

A short time later the black van crunched its way up the gravel driveway to the Benders' house. Vanessa came outside and walked over.

"What kept you guys?" she said.

"Sorry," Joe said. "We had a little delay."

"Somebody shot at us," Ms. Ziebarth said.

Vanessa's eyes grew big. "Is everybody okay?"

"Everybody's okay," Joe said.

"It happened so fast, by the time I realized what was going on, it was over," Ms. Ziebarth said.

"Shouldn't you call the police?" Vanessa asked.

"On a shooting incident like this we have to make a report in person," Frank said. "I guess we should head back to police headquarters and do that now."

As Ms. Ziebarth picked up the box containing her computer hard drive and got out of the van, she said to Vanessa, "I really can't thank you enough for letting me stay."

"It should be fun," Vanessa said, smiling. "What's in the box?"

"It's my hard drive," Ms. Ziebarth said. "I hope we can salvage the data."

"Hard drives these days are pretty tough," Vanessa said. "They're built to take a fair amount of abuse."

"Whether that includes surviving a gas explosion remains to be seen," Ms. Ziebarth said.

"My mom's got all kinds of equipment and programs," Vanessa said. "It shouldn't be too hard to recover your data."

"I'm hoping for the best."

"When it comes to computer troubleshooting, Vanessa *is* the best," Joe said.

Frank started up the van and said, "We'll call you later. If you're up to it, we can get something to eat." Joe waved goodbye as Frank backed the van out of the driveway to head back to town.

The Hardys arrived at police headquarters a short time later and were glad to find Officer Con Riley on duty. They told him about the shooting incident, giving him the exact time and location along with the description of the car and its license plate number. They also filled him in on the other incidents where Stevens was their main suspect.

"First he almost killed me with a pendulum to the head at the chemistry lab about ten minutes after we met him," Joe said.

"What chemistry lab?" Riley asked.

"Well . . ." Joe hesitated. Frank gave a barely noticeable shake of his head to say no, but Joe forged ahead. "It was Klingner's lab."

"What were you doing there?" Riley asked. "That should have been sealed off. Who gave you permission to go in?"

"Nobody really," Joe continued as Frank rolled his eyes. "We thought we might . . ."

"Snooping around a crime scene," Riley said. "You guys ought to know better. I don't care what you found, how did you plan to explain this to Detective Broussard?"

"Con, there's more," Joe said. "Stevens has been dogging us. Every time we try to corner him, we get ambushed. It's almost as if he's been trying to scare us off the case."

"We've got enough evidence on him for you to lock him up," Frank said.

"But what good is it if we can't use it officially?" Riley said.

"We just want you to have enough to hold him and charge him with something," Frank said.

"You guys know as well as I do, illegally obtained evidence won't hold up in court," Riley said.

"As long as it'll help solve the murder, we'll take the blame for the snooping," Frank said.

"Con, you've got to give it a shot," Joe said. "Listen, once you start questioning Stevens, he'll crack and probably confess to killing Klingner."

"Okay, okay," Riley said, taking a report form out of his desk and slipping it into his typewriter. "What else have you got?"

"Joe saw the red car leaving the chemistry department parking lot after he got hit with the pendulum," Frank said. "But the car got away."

"Then he threw a smoke bomb and tried to run us over in the high school parking lot the next day," Joe said.

"The same car?" Riley asked as he started to type the report.

"Same description," Joe said, "but we didn't

get the plate number. When we went to see him, he had a lame alibi about eating breakfast at home alone and listening to a classical music station. Then we think he followed us and smacked Frank on the head with a big chemistry book."

"Where was this?" Riley said.

"Ms. Ziebarth's apartment," Joe said.

"I hope you were invited in," Riley said.

"Not exactly," Joe said.

"That's what I was afraid of," Riley said. "By the time I finish filling out this report you two are going to be in almost as much trouble as Marcus Stevens." He paused to type some more then said, "So he got away again?"

Frank nodded. "We caught up with him in Professor Holt's lab," Frank said. "We were trying to get him to admit to the other attacks. He got really angry and stormed out. Next thing we knew, we were almost suffocating from poison gas. He probably set that up, too."

"Then he shot at us, only this time we finally got an ID on the car," Joe said.

"From what I hear, Stevens is an underage grad student who wears thick glasses and suspenders," Riley said. "Do you guys seriously think a guy like that is capable of mounting all these attacks?"

"I don't know," Frank said. "But he's smart, really smart."

Riley continued typing his report for a moment. Then he looked up and said, "So what's his motive?"

"We think it could be jealousy," Joe said. "He's very close to Ms. Ziebarth. She insists they're just friends, but it's pretty obvious that Stevens wishes there were more to it."

"Ms. Ziebarth claims Professor Klingner was going to take credit for some of her research," Frank said. "Stevens may have found out about that and thought he could avenge her by sabotaging Klingner."

"Or it could have been a professional motive," Joe said. "Ms. Ziebarth is trying to reconstruct her data. She thinks she can work out what's in there that could have been worth so much to Klingner and to whoever sabotaged him. In that case, maybe Stevens is working with that other graduate student, the one who disappeared."

"Who's that?" Riley asked.

"His name is Koo," Joe said.

"I don't know anything about him," Riley said. "Sounds like a lot of speculation, and most of your information seems to be coming from Ms. Ziebarth. She's still Detective Broussard's prime suspect. Of course you guys realize all of this information is going to have to go to Broussard."

"We know," said Joe. "But we're convinced it's going to lead to the real killer. Otherwise, we wouldn't have said anything."

"All right, now let's get back to the facts," Riley said. He asked them to confirm a few details about the shooting incident, checked them against what he'd typed on the report form, and then said, "Why don't we go outside and take a look at the van."

Outside, Con stared at the three neat holes in the door of the van. "Somebody was having target practice, and this door was the bull's-eye," he said. He pressed his right index finger into one hole. "Looks like a nine millimeter."

"The shots did come fast," Frank said, confirming that it could have been a semiautomatic. They went back inside, and Riley sat down at a computer terminal to run a check on the license plate number. He punched in the number as Frank and Joe stood looking over his shoulder. Within moments, information began appearing line by line on the screen.

"A red sedan," Con said, reading. "Make, model, year."

"And registered to—" Frank picked up.

The name *Stevens, Marcus* appeared in bright orange capitals followed by the address of Stevens's apartment building in Greenfield.

"Super-Nerd," Joe said.

"What was that?" Riley said to Joe.

"Oh, nothing," Joe said. "Just my pet nickname for him."

"Based on your report, we *can* put out a warrant for his arrest," Riley said. "Assault with a deadly weapon and suspicion of murder. As for right now, let's open up your door panels and get those bullets out. With any luck, we'll find a gun in Stevens's possession and match those bullets to it. Then we'll see if we can get him to volunteer any more information."

"I can't believe it," Yvonne Ziebarth said. "Marcus's car? You're positive?"

Joe, Frank, Callie, Vanessa, and Ms. Ziebarth were back at Mr. Pizza, sitting in a booth.

"That's right," Joe said. "They're going to arrest him for assault and question him about Klingner's murder."

"Couldn't someone else have stolen his car and be using it for these attacks?" Ms. Ziebarth asked.

"He would have reported it stolen," Joe said. "That would get him off the hook right away."

"Mild little Marcus," Ziebarth said, shaking her head. "I just don't believe it. And I won't—not until I hear it from Marcus himself."

"I've got some news, too," Callie said. "This afternoon I got the final results from the PIXE scan. The chemical on the label is, let's see," she said, consulting a small notepad, "disodium ethylenediaminetetraacetic acid."

"Disodium what?" Joe said.

"Disodium EDTA, for short," Ms. Ziebarth said.

Callie nodded. "We were hoping it would be uncommon enough so we could trace it to a few people. Well, unfortunately it's probably on everyone's hands on campus. Disodium EDTA is an ingredient in liquid hand soap—the kind stocked in every washroom at Bayport University."

"I guess that lead's a total washout," Joe said, causing everyone else at the table to grimace and roll their eyes.

The next day was Sunday, and Frank was on the phone first thing in the morning. He reached Officer Con Riley, who was on the weekend morning shift.

"How are you this morning, Con?" Frank asked. "I was wondering if there were any developments on Marcus Stevens."

"We picked him up last night," Riley said.

"That's great," Frank said. "Where'd you find him?"

"We had his house staked out, and when he pulled up we nabbed him. No sign of a gun in his car. He probably ditched it somewhere."

"Did he admit to anything?" Frank asked.

"I just told you everything I know," Riley said, "but I could patch you through to the detectives."

Frank wasn't too eager to talk with Detective Broussard, but before he could say anything to stop Riley from transferring his call he heard a click, then a ring followed by a familiar growl: "Homicide—Broussard."

"Uh, hello, Detective Broussard. Frank Hardy here. Congratulations on arresting Marcus Stevens. I know at least a few people who're glad he's off the streets. Joe and I were wondering, has he confessed yet?"

*"Confessed?"* Broussard exploded. "What is this? Your idea of a joke? If it is, it's a pretty sick one."

"No, sir," Frank said. "I just—"

"Confessed?" Broussard sputtered. "What's wrong with you kids? Can't you learn to mind your own business? Find some homework to do. Get an after-school job. Go play in traffic!

"For your information, Mr. Frank Hardy, Marcus Stevens *hasn't* confessed. No, as a matter of fact, we just had to let him go."

# Chapter

## 13

FRANK WAS STUNNED. "You had to let him go?" he said. "What happened?" There was a long pause.

Joe, who was sitting at the breakfast table, froze with a spoonful of cereal halfway to his mouth. "They let Stevens go? I don't believe it. How did it happen?" he mouthed.

Frank held up a finger to his mouth to silence Joe as he listened to Broussard sigh audibly.

"First of all, the report says you didn't actually see Stevens at the wheel," Broussard finally conceded. "And besides, Stevens has an alibi. So we couldn't hold him."

"What's his alibi?" Frank asked.

Joe got up so fast trying to put his ear to

the receiver to hear what Broussard was telling Frank that he jostled the table and knocked half a glass of milk on the floor.

"A parking receipt," Broussard said. "With the date and time stamped on it. The same time that you were being shot at, which proves Stevens wasn't the shooter."

"But anyone could forge one of those or touch up the time stamp," Frank said.

"Don't you think I know that?" Broussard said. "But try telling it to a judge. In the meantime, stay out of this investigation. I'm getting tired of telling you that. Don't call my office, and don't ask any more questions because you won't get any answers. In fact, interfere any more and so help me I'll arrest both you and your brother for obstructing justice." With that the detective slammed down the receiver.

"Did you hear that?" Frank said to Joe.

"I was trying," Joe said, sponging up the spilled milk.

"Stevens has an alibi," Frank said. "A parking receipt. It could be bogus, but there's nothing the cops can do."

"Is that all Broussard told you?"

"I'm lucky he told me anything," Frank said.

"So now Stevens is on the loose," Joe said, "and Ms. Ziebarth's out at Vanessa's. Maybe we should drive out to check on them."

"Guess what, Joe?" Frank said. "There's a

new invention. It's called a telephone. Why don't you just call them up?"

Joe shook his head. "Stevens could be waiting to pounce out there, and they'd never know."

"How could Stevens even find the Benders' place?" Frank said.

"Do you remember when we were at Stevens's apartment the other day and Ms. Ziebarth was there?" Joe asked. "She had her class roster with all the students' addresses and phone numbers. Stevens could have taken a peek."

"But how would he connect Vanessa with where Ms. Ziebarth is now?"

Joe's face went red. "We were almost all the way there when he shot at us," he said. "Frank, we can't afford to take Stevens lightly anymore. He could be responsible for killing Thomas Klingner, ransacking Ms. Ziebarth's apartment, rigging that gas explosion, and shooting at us. Who knows what he'll try next?"

Frank held up his hands in surrender. "All right, all right. You win. Let's take a drive."

A short time later the Hardys pulled slowly off the main road near the Benders' farm. Frank and Joe scanned the area for anything unusual—fresh tire marks on the driveway, flattened grass where a car might have parked to wait in ambush. But they saw nothing.

The Hardys drove up to the house. Vanessa's car was parked on one side of the barn entrance and her mother's on the other. No other vehicles were in sight.

"To what do we owe this pleasure?" called a voice. Holding a tray with an empty pitcher and glasses, Vanessa had just stepped out of her mother's animation studio in the old barn. "You guys just missed the last of the iced tea, but there's soda."

"Hi, Vanessa," said Joe as the brothers climbed down from the van. "No thanks, we're fine. We were just in the neighborhood so we thought we'd drop by."

"Just in the neighborhood?" Vanessa responded with a knowing smile. "Well, I'd hate to think you two were looking in on us, thinking we can't take care of ourselves."

"Oh, never," Joe said with a quick grin.

"Ms. Ziebarth is in the studio. We've been working on the hard drive since breakfast. I guess we could use a short break." Setting the tray on the porch, she turned and led the brothers into the barn.

In the converted space was a wall of large color monitors, long counters with digital editing equipment and sound-mixing machines, and computers on gleaming metal shelves.

In the middle of it all, Yvonne Ziebarth sat

at a large desk with a monitor and keyboard in front of her. She was obviously poring over her data.

"Hi, Joe. Hi, Frank," she said, turning at the sound of their voices.

"How's it going?" Joe asked.

"Slowly," she said. "It turns out there was a fair amount of jumbled data. Vanessa's been recovering it, and I'm going over it."

"It isn't hard, but it's time-consuming," Vanessa said, taking her place at another keyboard. "We're checking each file individually, then running bad sectors through a repair program."

"Any idea how much longer?" asked Frank.

"Another day's work, I'd say," replied Vanessa.

"You know," Ziebarth said, "seeing all my research from start to finish like this puts it in a whole new light. I'm thinking about all the new directions my experiments could take."

"I guess we should let you get back to work, then," Frank said. "No point in hanging around and distracting you."

"There's one more thing before we leave," Joe said. "We talked with Detective Broussard this morning. They picked up Marcus Stevens last night but they let him go."

"He had this flaky-sounding alibi," Frank continued. "Broussard said it might not hold up in court, but they had to buy it for now."

"I told you yesterday I don't think he's the killer," Ziebarth said.

"Wait a minute," Vanessa said. "Then that *is* why you two came out here today. To protect us from Marcus Stevens, right?"

"Vanessa," Joe said, acting shocked. "How could you think something like that? Come on, Frank, let's get out of here. Who knows what she'll accuse us of next."

As they drove down the Benders' driveway to where it joined the main thoroughfare, Joe said, "Frank, have you got anything special planned today?"

Frank glanced sideways at his brother. They reached the tiny intersection, and he slowed the van to a stop. "What's on your mind?" Frank said.

"You said you have a calculus quiz tomorrow, right?" Joe said. "Well, I threw your book bag and some of my books in back. What if we just kind of parked in those woods there and studied awhile?"

"In the woods?" Frank said. "In the shadows maybe, where the van will blend in and you can keep an eye on the road here?"

Joe shrugged, then smiled.

Frank sighed as he pulled the van over so he could back in among the trees. "I do need to study for that quiz, and I guess here's as good a place as any," he said.

\*     \*     \*

The Hardys met at their lockers in the hallway after school the next day. Frank put some books on the shelf of his locker, then stopped to stretch and rub his back.

"Joe, the next time you want to sit in the van for seven hours on a Sunday, count me out," Frank said. He groaned and raised his arms overhead, cracking his back.

"Okay, but how'd you do on your quiz?" Joe said.

"I think I aced it."

"There you go," Joe said. "Don't say I never do you any favors."

"Are you ready to go?" Frank asked, wincing at the stiffness in his shoulders.

"I'm going to stick around," Joe said. He tossed the van keys to Frank, who snagged them neatly out of the air. "There's an experiment I need to work on."

"Would that be a chemistry experiment? And where's Ms. Ziebarth going to be?"

Joe smiled. "Okay, you got me. She'll be here, too. She's staying late to grade papers."

"And this gives you another chance to keep an eye on her," Frank said.

"Seriously, Frank," Joe said, "Stevens knows where she works. If he's planning another attack, this would be the perfect time and place—after school, when the building's fairly deserted."

"Joe, you can't watch her twenty-four hours a day," Frank said.

"I know, but Stevens is bound to tip his hand soon," Joe said. "Maybe we can nab him this time."

"Have fun," Frank said. "I'm headed out to the Benders' to help with the data recovery."

"Sounds good," Joe said. "I'll catch a ride over with Ms. Ziebarth."

Frank grinned. "That way you get to play guardian angel door-to-door."

It was almost five o'clock before Joe and Ms. Ziebarth walked to her car in the nearly deserted Bayport High parking lot. Before long, they were moving along at a good clip in light traffic. It was a warm, sunny evening, there was a pleasant breeze blowing, and they had the windows rolled down—perfect late spring weather in Bayport.

"Thanks again for the ride," Joe said as they headed out of town.

"Hm?" Ms. Ziebarth said.

"I said I appreciate the ride, Ms. Ziebarth."

"My pleasure, Joe," she said. "Sorry if I seem distracted, but I was just thinking about my research. Thanks to you and Frank for all your help. You got me out of a real jam. But you really don't have to watch over me anymore. I'm not worried about Marcus's being out of jail. I probably know him better than anybody does."

While Joe was listening to Ms. Ziebarth he was also looking through the windshield of the car. It was a little dirty, he thought. He squinted and noticed some strange smudges right in his line of vision. The more he looked at them, the more they looked like handprints.

If there was one thing Joe hated, it was a dirty windshield. He wondered if Ms. Ziebarth felt the same way.

"Ms. Ziebarth," Joe said, "can you see out the windshield? It looks kind of dirty on my side."

"You're right, Joe," she said. "It looks like somebody smudged it all over. I didn't notice it this morning."

Ms. Ziebarth twisted the wiper-washer lever on the steering column. Liquid squirted onto the glass, and the wipers jumped to life. It wasn't the usual clear, thin, bluish fluid, though. It was something gray colored and gritty looking, which the wipers immediately smeared across the windshield.

The next instant, before their disbelieving eyes, the windshield suddenly transformed itself into a mirror so that Ms. Ziebarth and Joe sat staring at their own amazed reflections.

"Joe," Ms. Ziebarth cried as they hurtled along. "I can't see where we're going!"

# Chapter

## 14

Yvonne Ziebarth's first reaction was to slam on the brakes. Her tires screeched, and as her little sedan suddenly slowed, a deafening horn blasted behind them. Joe spun and saw a semitrailer bearing down fast, its headlights flashing frantically.

"The truck can't brake this fast," Joe barked. "Just keep going—hold the wheel straight." Ms. Ziebarth gripped the wheel, moved her hands directly in front of her, and hit the gas. The car jumped forward. The huge trailer behind them fishtailed as the driver hit the air brakes.

Joe stuck his head out the window to navigate for Ms. Ziebarth. The wind whipped his hair back, and he had to narrow his eyes to slits to see the road. They were near the end of a straightaway with no cars immediately ahead. There was a sharp bend ahead, though, so they'd have to make a move fast. Joe spotted a flat, open area to the right just before the curve. He figured that if they timed it right, they could skid to a stop right there.

"Keep going straight," Joe shouted back over his shoulder, the wind almost swallowing his voice. "Hit the brakes and turn right—*now!*"

He grabbed the window frame to brace himself as the car whipped sharply right and bounced when it hit the shoulder. They skidded into the open area with a violent thump and bounce. Ms. Ziebarth stomped the brake with both feet, and the car started to spin on the dirt, slowing and, with a final jolt, it came to a stop. Dust swirled in through Joe's window, and the trailer truck roared off with a brief double-toot on its air horn.

After a slight pause, Ms. Ziebarth said, "I guess we made it."

Joe realized he was still gripping the window frame with whitened fingers. He slowly opened them and let go. He could see his own mirror-like reflection in the windshield and said, "What is that stuff?"

They climbed out. The thick metal guardrail was just two feet from the front fender, and Joe shook his head. "That was too close for comfort," he said.

The car sat straddling a rut, its front tires on one side, its rear ones on the other. One back tire had blown out and shredded. Ms. Ziebarth bent over to examine the windshield. With a fingernail she scratched at the shiny silvery crust and saw it crumble, leaving a clear spot of bare glass through which she could see into the car.

"Is it paint?" Joe asked.

"No," Ziebarth said. "Paint wouldn't dry so quickly. The wipers would have cleaned it off, or at least smeared it. Actually, I don't think paint could be squirted through the wiper-fluid nozzles. They're too tiny. No, this seems to be a coating of silver oxide particles."

"Silver oxide?"

"It's used in photographic film," she explained. "When the particles are exposed to light, they react—well, I won't get technical. All you need to know is that light turns them silver. Let's pop open the hood.

"The windshield washer fluid is right over there," she said, pointing to a plastic container with a tube running from its side. Joe unscrewed the lid and Ms. Ziebarth bent down to sniff what was inside.

"Whew," she said. "That smells like pentane. It's very volatile, quick to evaporate." She peered inside the container. "Take a look."

Joe looked in and saw particles the size of pepper grains swirling slowly around.

"It's ingenious," Ms. Ziebarth said. "Someone drained the regular washer fluid and substituted a mixture of pentane and silver oxide particles. The vibration of the car kept the particles from settling. But when the solution was sprayed onto the windshield, the pentane dried instantly, leaving a silver oxide coating. As soon as the sun hit the particles, they turned silver."

"And we had a mirror instead of a windshield," Joe said. "Whoever did it smudged the windshield first to be sure you'd have to use the spray and wipers," Joe added.

Ziebarth smiled. "Brilliant." Joe thought she seemed so impressed that maybe she was forgetting about their near-crash.

"There's a gas station up ahead," Joe said. "We can walk there and call a tow truck."

Before trudging off down the road, they stopped for a moment. Joe gazed down at their reflections in the windshield of the dusty white sedan. "Ms. Ziebarth," he said, "I guess you're not still wondering if someone's out to get you now, are you?"

He didn't need to wait for an answer.

An hour later Joe called Vanessa's house from the pay phone at the gas station where Ms. Ziebarth's car had been towed.

Frank got on the line. "We had some excitement on the way over," Joe said. "I'll tell you about it later. The thing is, we want Ms. Ziebarth's car checked out. We're at Harry's Service Station just off Hodges Road."

Frank was there with the van in ten minutes. On the way to the Benders', they filled him in on their adventure. Once they arrived at the farm, Joe told the story all over again to Vanessa. Then Frank and Joe agreed their best move was to try to track down Marcus Stevens.

"Whoever's planning these attacks knows a lot about chemistry," Frank said. "And unless we can figure out where Koo is, Marcus is our best candidate."

"Maybe Super-Nerd One will lead us to Super-Nerd Two," Joe said.

"In any case, I'm interested to hear Number One's reaction to the mirrored windshield story," Frank said.

"I'd like his opinion about yesterday's shooting, too," Joe said. "The police may have talked to him about it, but we haven't."

"Let's try the university again," Frank said.

"But he was fired, remember?" Joe said.

"That shouldn't matter," Ms. Ziebarth cut in. "It just means he's not Holt's assistant anymore. He's still a grad student. The chem department is basically his second home. If you hang around there, you'll find him eventually."

"I think I'll stay and finish with the data recovery," Vanessa said. "Besides, it's my turn to take care of Ms. Ziebarth for a while."

With that, Vanessa and Ms. Ziebarth exchanged amused looks, rolled their eyes, and wished Frank and Joe luck in finding their favorite chemistry grad student.

By the time the Hardys arrived at the science building, it was early evening. They had stopped at a fast-food stand for hamburgers and fries.

"I don't see Stevens's car," Joe said, as they chose a spot in one corner of the parking lot.

Frank checked his watch. "It's dinnertime," he said. "Maybe he went out to eat."

The Hardys sat in the van and watched and waited. After about an hour, Joe spotted Stevens's car. "Frank, it's him."

The familiar red sedan pulled into the lot from the far entrance and slipped into a parking space. As they reached for their door handles, the Hardys watched Stevens start to climb out of his car, then abruptly stop.

"Hold it, Joe," Frank said. "What's he looking at?"

"He looks surprised. What could surprise him in his own car?"

"I don't know," Frank said, "but let's hang back a second."

Stevens picked up something off the floor of his car. He hunched over, turning the object in his hand to examine it. Then he glanced up sharply, as if to see if anyone was watching. Stevens slipped the mysterious object into his pocket, shut his car door, and hurried to the science building.

"Come on," Frank said, and they followed Stevens inside. As they entered the ground floor hallway, they caught a glimpse of him boarding an elevator. On a hunch, they rushed up the stairs to the third floor and peeked through the small window in the stairwell door. Stevens was letting himself into Holt's lab.

"He probably kept a copy of the keys after he got fired," Joe whispered.

As Stevens went into the lab, the Hardys slipped past the stairwell door, careful not to slam it behind them. They moved quickly and quietly to the lab door, and Joe grabbed it just before it clicked shut. Stevens had gone straight into Professor Holt's private office. Without thinking, Joe rushed in after him.

"Hold it, Joe," Frank whispered, but it was too late. Joe charged headlong through the lab and shoved his way into the office behind Stevens.

The grad student whirled around to face Joe with both arms outstretched. In a solid two-handed grip, he was pointing a shiny nickel-plated automatic pistol straight at Joe's forehead.

# Chapter

## 15

ALL RIGHT, MARCUS, just take it easy," Joe said.

Frank appeared at the door, crouched and ready for action. "Drop the gun, now!" he barked. "Shoot either of us and the other one will be all over you before you can blink."

Stevens didn't hesitate. He lowered his arms and held the pistol out to Joe in the palm of one hand. "Here, take it," he said. "I don't want it. It's yours, isn't it?"

Joe snatched the gun from Stevens and set it down on the desk. "Ours? What are you talking about?"

"I thought you planted it. I never saw it until five minutes ago when I was parking my car," Stevens said. "I got out of the car and saw it lying on the floor. I guess I stopped a little too fast and it slid out from under the seat. I have no idea how it got there."

Joe glanced at Frank. Another far-fetched story from Super-Nerd, he thought. The funny thing was, he made a pretty convincing liar.

"If it's not your gun, why were you so quick to pull it on Joe?" Frank asked.

"I heard someone barge in behind me," Stevens said. "I had the gun in my hand. What would you have done?"

"Probably deliver a spinning wheel kick to the solar plexus," Frank said, "but in your case that might not have been an option."

"So what's the idea of snooping around Professor Holt's office?" Joe said.

Stevens began to reach into his pocket.

"Watch it, Frank," Joe said, taking a step toward Stevens. "He may have another weapon."

"No, no," Stevens said. "It's just a note, see?" He brought out a folded slip of paper. "It's E-mail that came fifteen minutes ago on my home machine." He handed it to Joe. "I printed it out."

Joe read aloud, " 'Meet me at Holt's office. Seven P.M.' It's from Tang Ly Koo." The brothers glanced at the wall clock—it was a couple of minutes after seven.

"I've been trying to contact him ever since he disappeared," Stevens said. "I've been leaving notes, phone messages, faxes, E-mail. But no answer. Then I got that note, and I realized this might be my big chance to nab him. I also thought it might be a trap, so when I found the gun, I brought it with me."

"Didn't you think you were in over your head, Marcus?" Joe said. "Sneaking into this lab with a gun for a secret meeting with a fugitive?"

"Well, now that the big experts are here, maybe we can crack the case wide open," he said, his voice dripping with sarcasm.

"Easy does it, guys," Frank said. "It's after seven," he said, glancing at his watch, "and no sign of Koo."

"Why would he bother sending that message if he wasn't going to show up?" asked Stevens.

"I have no idea," Frank said. "Unless he wanted to send us on a wild-goose chase."

"Since we're here, why don't we take a look around?" Joe suggested. "Marcus was good enough to open the door for us so we might as well take advantage of it. Maybe we can find some information on Koo or his whereabouts." Joe turned to Stevens. "Marcus, why don't you make yourself useful and help us out?"

The threesome began searching the office, looking inside, around, and under everything— file cabinets, desk drawers, bookshelves, the closet. They even peeked behind the framed diplomas and pictures on the walls and started checking all the textbooks for loose papers. Then they started checking the papers from Holt's desk. After a few minutes Joe held up what looked like some kind of official form. "I wonder why Professor Holt would be into something like this," he said.

Frank took the form, glanced at it, and said, "It's a receipt. Holt applied to the motor vehicle department for a vanity plate."

"Vanity plate?" Stevens said.

"You know, those personalized license plates," Frank said. "They say stuff like BIG-JOHN or GOLFPRO."

"It doesn't show what he wants on the plates," Joe said. "Probably something like CHEMNERD. How's that sound, Marcus?"

Stevens pretended to be concentrating hard on a sheaf of papers he was reading.

A few minutes later Frank said, "Hey, here's something." He had noticed there was a disk in the floppy drive of the personal computer on Holt's desk. He punched the Eject button on the drive, pulled out the disk, and took a look at the label.

"It's in Chinese," Frank said.

"It must be Koo's," Joe said.

Frank flipped the computer on. "Let's see if we can make any sense of it," he said.

"I'll try E-mailing Tang again," Stevens said.

"Who knows, maybe he's on a machine somewhere."

There was a sharp rap on the door, and all three turned quickly around. Joe was reaching for the door handle when Vanessa and Yvonne Ziebarth rushed in.

"Great," Vanessa said. "You guys are here."

"And you found Marcus," Ms. Ziebarth said. "We have some exciting news. I finished reviewing all my research data. Remember how I said it might all start to fall into place if I took some more time with it? Well, I just came across something big. I can hardly believe I didn't see it from the start. I guess I just didn't have the experience. But Professor Klingner must have, which is probably why he took credit for my work and why he got killed."

"You know why Klingner was murdered?" Joe asked.

"I have a pretty good idea," said Ziebarth.

"Then you must also know who killed him," Frank said.

"Correct," she said. "At least, I'm ninety-five percent sure,"

"Only ninety-five percent?" repeated a familiar but oddly muffled voice at the door.

Everyone turned to behold a chilling sight. In the doorway stood a figure in a white lab coat with the huge buglike eyes, black rubber snout, and crisscrossing elastic straps of a gas mask covering his face. His hands were sheathed in large yellow rubber gloves. They held a red metal canister with a label that said Danger—Phosgene.

"Shall we make it an even one hundred percent?" the voice asked.

# Chapter

## 16

FOR A MOMENT everyone just stood there, struck silent in amazement. Frank thought he recognized the voice through the gas mask. Then, when he noticed the figure was wearing a bow tie, he was sure.

"It's Dr. Holt," Frank said.

The figure paused, then stepped into the room, pulling the door closed behind him. He held the safety can at waist level, one yellow-gloved hand gripping the cap. The slightest twist of his wrist would fill the room with toxic gas.

"You guessed correctly," Dr. Holt said, his voice still muffled but recognizable. "Not that it'll do you much good."

"You killed Professor Klingner," Ms. Ziebarth said. "You'll never get away with it while I'm still alive."

Holt nodded and said, "That was my thought, exactly, Ms. Ziebarth. Tell me, how far have you gotten with your research? Did you finally figure out where it was leading?"

Ms. Ziebarth smiled coolly. "As a matter of fact, I think I have," she said. "In a way, you did me a favor by arranging that gas explosion. I'm right, aren't I? That blast was your work?"

Holt gave a little nod to accept credit.

Ziebarth went on. "Because of the explosion, I was forced to reconstruct my research. It gave me a chance to review all my data, and that's how I figured out where it was heading. Then it became obvious why Klingner thought it was so valuable." Ms. Ziebarth glared at the masked man. "It had to do with how electricity is stored. It's a possible Nobel prize–winning breakthrough. Klingner was going to take credit for it. It must have tied in to your experiments somehow," she said to Holt.

Holt nodded. "Quite correct. What you and Klingner were working on would have interfered with my invention." Behind his mask, the professor's voice trembled with excitement. "I have devised the first clean battery."

"A clean battery?" Stevens said. "But that's impossible."

"Maybe impossible for *you* to imagine," Holt said, "but I've done it."

"What's a clean battery?" Vanessa asked.

"When you throw it out, it doesn't pollute the environment," Joe explained. "Most dead batteries are dumped into landfills. The chemicals in them eventually leak into the ground, contaminating water sources. Imagine how much pollution comes from all the batteries from kids' toys, personal stereos, laptop computers, cordless phones, flashlights, and cameras—not to mention cars."

"Batteries by the billions," Holt confirmed. "Almost three billion thrown away last year alone and that's just by Americans, a small percentage of the world's total population."

"A nonpolluting battery would be an incredible breakthrough," Stevens said.

"And when the right manufacturer buys my patent," Holt added, "it will earn me a fortune."

"But how does it work?" Joe asked.

"I began with bacteria," Holt said. "Anaerobic bacteria, which require no oxygen and therefore could survive inside a sealed battery container. True, they'd produce methane as a by-product, but I have a second kind of bacteria that could consume it."

"But where does the electricity come in?" asked Frank.

"A stroke of brilliance,'" Holt boasted. "I'd been experimenting with DNA from creatures that produce electricity—deep-sea fish that glow, fireflies, moray eels. My all-natural battery combines anaerobic bacteria with electricity-producing cells. Not only will it be clean, but it will last ten times longer than ordinary batteries. It will also be recyclable, since the case is aluminum."

"Wow," Joe mused, "clean, long-lasting batteries. That could change the future."

"I'm terribly sorry, young man," Holt said, "but because of your meddlesome ways you won't live to see the future. I'm now forced to kill all of you by opening this phosgene canister, which I can assure you is correctly labeled. Don't worry, there's enough in here so that the pain will last only a couple of seconds—a brief searing of your lungs and then goodbye for eternity. After it's all over, I'll put the canister in your hands, Stevens, making it look as though you went out in a blaze of glory, taking everyone in this office with you."

"But why did you kill Dr. Klingner?" Frank asked. "Did he find out? Did you kill him to keep him quiet?"

"Klingner was getting close," Holt said. "The fool bragged to me that he was about to announce a major breakthrough in energy transfer that could have significant applications for batteries. It was child's play for me to figure out the rest."

"So you murdered him," Ziebarth said.

"To slow down his research I relabeled the

phosgene knowing it would kill the anaerobic bacteria in his experiment. I had to delay his work long enough for me to take full advantage of my invention. Did I know Klingner would die?" Holt shrugged. "No. After all, I couldn't foresee exactly how much, if any, of the gas he might inhale during his experiments."

"But knowing the phosgene could kill a human being," Joe said, "you took a chance with his life and he died."

"A minor complication," Holt said, "but we scientists are used to them.

"Considering Klingner tried to steal your research," he said to Ziebarth, "I'm surprised you're not grateful to me for killing him."

"Klingner was wrong," Ziebarth said, "but he didn't deserve to die for it. No, I don't thank you, Dr. Holt. In my book you're still a murderer."

"And to cover your trail," Joe said, "you framed Ms. Ziebarth. Her argument with Klingner gave you the perfect opportunity. You faked the message from Klingner asking her to come to the lab so witnesses could place her there on the day he died. You typed the phony oxygen label on her computer and threw away the backing. Even if someone found it, which we did, you figured it was evidence that could be used against her."

Professor Holt addressed the Hardys. "Your meddling ruined the case against her and allowed her to continue her research. You forced me to try to eliminate her altogether."

Ziebarth asked, "But why did you try to hire me?"

"Two reasons," Frank answered. "He could keep an eye on your research and he could keep you so busy doing his work you wouldn't have any time for your own."

Joe glared at the masked man. "And besides arranging the gas explosion at her apartment," he said, "you tried to run down Frank and me, and you put that silver oxide solution in Ms. Ziebarth's wiper fluid."

"Your deductive powers are impressive," Holt said. "You would have made a good scientist—not that you'll get the chance now."

Suddenly Stevens snatched the gun from the table and aimed it at Holt.

"Don't move, Dr. Holt!" he shouted.

Holt just laughed; it was a hollow sound behind the mask. "Sorry, Marcus, but you don't quite make it as a hero," he said, and made a move in Stevens's direction.

Stevens closed his eyes and squeezed the trigger. The gun clicked harmlessly.

"The gun is empty, you twit." Holt sneered.

"How did you know that?" Ms. Ziebarth asked.

"Because I planted it in Stevens's car after I fired it at that black van of yours. I meant for the police to find it. Unfortunately, as it turned out, they searched his car before I had a chance to plant the gun."

"But how did you get Stevens's car?" asked Callie.

"He didn't," Frank said. "That's where the vanity license plate comes in. He got a plate very close to Stevens's, then changed one letter. It's easy to make an *F* into an *E* or an *8* into a *3*. Then you rent a car with the same make, model, and color and put the plates on it."

"Not bad for an amateur detective," Holt said. "I recommend Arnie's Auto Rental. They have the widest selection in town.

"Now, boys and girls, I have one final question for you," Holt said. "Why did you all come here?"

As if in answer to the professor, a knock sounded at the door behind him. He spun quickly and pulled open the door. There, framed in the doorway, stood Tang Ly Koo, appearing surprised and confused.

Koo's appearance was enough of a diversion for Frank and Joe. Without hesitating, they sprung into action. Frank unleashed a flying karate kick at the sturdy metal canister in Professor Holt's hands, sending it flying across the room. Holt turned toward Frank, but before he could take a step, Joe threw himself hard at the masked man, taking him down in a flying body tackle and pinning him to the floor.

Holt fought back but Joe was able to put the professor in a hammerlock. Then Frank twisted his right arm behind his back and he gave up. Meanwhile, Ms. Ziebarth got on the office phone and called 911. The Bayport police arrived within minutes, handcuffed Holt, and read him his rights.

After the cops led Holt away, the Hardys turned their attention to Koo. "Why did you run away if you had nothing to hide?" Joe asked him.

Koo seemed embarrassed. "I must admit, when Dr. Holt told me my presence in the lab would indeed require me to be questioned by the police, I became very frightened. In my country, you see, people questioned by the authorities in a murder are quite often never seen again. So, with a thousand apologies, I thought it best to disappear until the killer was apprehended."

"But how did you know to send a message to Stevens regarding Holt?" Joe asked.

"When I fled, I packed my things so hurriedly that I accidentally mixed up two computer disks. I left one that was mine"—Koo nodded at the disk Frank had found—"and took one of Dr. Holt's instead. On it was a letter from Dr. Holt to a commercial concern saying he guaranteed he could buy some time against competing interests and could deliver his formulas." Koo shrugged. "The computer

revealed this file was dated *before* Dr. Klingner's death. Of course, that is when I decided
it was time to contact my friend Marcus by
electronic mail."

"That could explain why Professor Holt ran-
sacked Ms. Ziebarth's apartment," Joe said.
"He was searching for his missing disk."

Stevens turned to Joe and swallowed hard.
"Now that this is all over," he said, "I guess I
should apologize for all the stuff I did do. Like
whacking you on the head with that pendulum
and everything."

Joe looked at Stevens, cocked his head as if
he were trying to decide whether to accept the
apology or not, then said nothing.

Ms. Ziebarth broke the silence. "Well,
guys," she said. "I can't say I'm unhappy our
little adventure is over, but I think it has
helped decide one thing. I'm going back to
school to finish my Ph.D." Smiling, she turned
to Tang Ly Koo. "I'm also going to bet you
ten dollars I win a Nobel prize before you do."

Koo grinned and stuck out his hand. "You
have a deal," he said as the two of them shook
on it.

"It looks like you're the one who loses out,
Joe," Frank said. "With Ms. Ziebarth going
back to grad school, where does that leave
your chemistry grades?"

"I've got some free time next semester,"

Stevens said. "I could be available for tutoring."

Joe shook his head and said, "I'll tell you what, Marcus. I'll accept your apology—but only on the condition that you never mention the word *chemistry* to me again. Over the last few days, I think I've had enough of it to last me a lifetime."

Frank and Joe make a special trip to Bayport
Fairgrounds to check out the steeplechase races.
They want to catch the champion horse Against All
Odds in action. He's ahead of the race and on form
until an unexpected injury pulls him suddenly out of
the running. It seems a saboteur has struck and
when, soon afterwards, the stallion disappears, the
brothers suspect it's more than a case of simple
horse-rustling they have to deal with. Whoever took
Against All Odds is a master of deception, diversion
and even . . . death!